Undeni

J. S.

Print ISBNs
Amazon print 9780228630906
Ingram Spark 9780228630890
Barnes & Noble 9780228630883
BWL Print 9780228630876

B.W.L. Publishing Inc.

Books we love to write …
Authors around the world.

http://bwlpublishing.ca

Acknowledgements

BWL Publishing acknowledges the Province of Alberta for their ongoing support through the Alberta Publisher's Cultural Industry Operating Grant.

Alberta
Government

Table of Contents

Chapter 1

Stunned by the long lineup extending from the snowy parking lot to the waiting area of the remote Ontario hospital, Dr. Zachary Auckerman headed toward the nurses' station.

The head nurse who'd welcomed him to Ojibson the previous evening discussed triage with a nurse wearing colorful scrubs depicting Snow White and the Seven Dwarfs.

"Hello, Angela." Zachary unzipped his winter coat. "Hello, Snow White."

The younger nurse chortled. "I'm Camille, Dr. Auckerman, but feel free to call me Sleepy." The amusement in her voice blended with a lovely French-Canadian accent.

"Nice meeting you, Nurse *Sleepy*. I'm *Doc*." For the first time since he dared speak the truth, Zachary felt welcomed. "Who are all these people?"

The northern community of roughly one thousand people needed a doctor, and although he'd already signed his contract,

7

Zachary didn't officially start working for another few days.

"The news of your arrival spread overnight. I know you're not scheduled to see any patients yet, but no one told them when they started lining up before dawn." Nurse Angela cast an apologizing gaze over the crowd. "Many residents haven't seen a real doctor since Dr. Holloway died of a heart attack four years ago. They're desperate, but also hopeful you'll stay."

People stared or threw sideways glances in Zachary's direction, and the murmur in the lineup intensified. His identity was being unmasked.

He'd come to meet the staff and familiarize himself with the layout of the hospital before spending the rest of the day unpacking and going grocery shopping. However, the expectant looks on his new patients' faces called for a change of plans.

Zachary squared his shoulders and turned toward the lineup. "Good morning, everyone." Silence fell on the waiting area the instant he started speaking. "I'm Zachary Auckerman, your new town doctor. Nurse Angela will begin triage starting with..." His gaze fell upon a toddler dressed in a neon yellow snowsuit and hugging tight to the leg of a heavily pregnant woman. "With the mother ready to deliver her little one in public." The mother-to-be waddled toward him, eliciting chuckles from the crowd. "I will only see emergencies today, but the nurses will take appointments. I'm looking forward to greeting each one of you in the days and weeks to come."

"You're a glutton for punishment, Doctor, but well done." Nurse Angela handed him a digital tablet. "Susan's medical record. It's her fourth child. I'll take her into Exam Room One."

* * *

"Nana, there's no doctor performing secret surgeries in the basement." Arguing was pointless, but Willow Mitchell refused to feed her eighty-four-year-old grandmother's delusion.

A commodity as hot as a doctor would be besieged by a pack of desperate patients within seconds of stepping into the nursing home. The physician wouldn't stand a chance of reaching the noisy service elevator leading to the basement.

"I saw him at the top of the ladder." Anger coated Nana's words. "He wore scrubs."

Willow muffled a sigh. On good days, Nana trudged down the corridor with her walker. The rest of the time she sat in a rocking chair or slept in bed. She couldn't climb a single step without falling, but she could have seen an attendant on a ladder and mistaken him for her imaginary doctor. All the attendants and nurses wore shabby scrubs, except for the creepy male nurse hired six months ago.

"Why don't you take a nap, Nana?" Answering her grandmother's call while fixing a toilet tank had been a mistake. Willow needed to finish the job before her client's children returned from school and asked to use the only bathroom in the house. "I'll come visit you tonight."

"Don't treat me like a lunatic child, Brigitte."

The name that her grandmother spat out spoke of her failing mind. Still, it jabbed an invisible knife in Willow's heart. Dealing with Nana had become a dreaded chore.

"I have to go, Nana." Willow shoved her phone into the waterproof pocket of her work coveralls before sticking her hands back into the empty toilet tank.

Water was leaking from one of the rusty bolts holding the tank in place, so she'd unscrewed the left one and replaced it with a shiny new bolt, but the right bolt refused to budge.

"Come on..." Crammed between an old-fashioned cast-iron claw foot tub and a white vanity, she once again tightened her grip and tugged, only to give up moments later. The recalcitrant nut was fused to the bolt, leaving Willow no other option than to saw it off.

Unlike her bolt cutter, her smallest saw fit under the tank, but the angle of the blade prevented her from seeing the bolt. Using her fingers, Willow felt the nut. The rust had distorted the grooves. She positioned the blade as flush as possible underneath the nut, and careful not to damage the back wall, she sawed back and forth. A few inches forth, a few inches back.

After a few minutes, she paused to feel the bolt. The indentation she made was as shallow as her fingernails were short. Resigned to a slow and laborious progression, she resumed sawing while keeping her left hand near the bolt.

The blade skidded.

Scorching pain traveled along her nerve endings. "Pooping hell."

* * *

Standing in front of the bathroom sink, Willow peeled the duct tape strapped around her wrist and winced.

After her mishap, she'd wrapped a clean gauze around her hand then donned two disposable gloves to prevent infection while she finished the job. Sealing the gloves around her wrist had sounded like a reasonable course of action at the time, but she hadn't anticipated it would also lead to a painful waxing.

Pulling on the tape ripped the gloves. They came off splashing red droplets on the white porcelain.

The cotton gauze was soaked with blood. "This can't be good."

A nurse had once told her to keep adding layers to a bleeding injury until it could be properly treated. Heeding the advice, Willow wrapped a facecloth over the bloody gauze. She hadn't planned on spending the evening, or the night, at the hospital waiting for a nurse to stitch her hand, but she didn't have a choice. The bleeding had to stop.

Her phone rang. The name on the screen further dampened her mood. An early evening call from the nursing home could only mean two things. A pipe burst or her grandmother flipped.

Swallowing her frustration, Willow answered. "Yes?"

"Hello, Mitch. It's Elisabeth." Like everyone else in town, the director of her grandmother's nursing home called her Mitch. "Could you spare me fifteen minutes this evening? We need to talk about your grandmother."

Elisabeth Brown wouldn't have requested Willow's presence at such short notice unless the situation was grave.

"I'll be there in ten minutes." Willow had to drive by the nursing home to get to the hospital, so she might as well stop there first.

* * *

Willow paced Elisabeth's office, skeptical of her recommendations.

"Nurse Darius examined her, Mitch." A thin woman in her fifties, Elisabeth sat with her back straight in a padded armchair behind an old wooden desk. "He assured me that increasing her meds will help with her mental and physical decline."

Help who, Elisabeth? Nana or your creepy nurse? Unflattering rumors abounded about Nurse Darius Wiedrich. Willow wouldn't let him approach her with a ten-foot pole to treat her bleeding hand. Still, she swallowed her frustration before words she might regret escaped her mouth. "I know Nana is experiencing serious health issues. That's why I was forced to place her here." If Willow could have afforded to hire a reliable care attendant, she would have kept her grandmother at home. "How about giving me a record of her current medications, and the changes you recommend, then I'll look into it."

The director stared at her from above the pewter rim of oval glasses. "I know you're her guardian, Mitch, but you do realize her record contains lots of scientific terms, right?"

Irked by the condescending remark, Willow paused in front of the desk. "I'll visit Nana for ten minutes, Elisabeth. That should give you ample time to fulfill my request."

* * *

Upon entering her grandmother's room on the second floor, Willow glanced into the bathroom.

Someone had tossed a blue towel into the toilet.

Willow sighed picking it up, then threw it in the tub. Nothing else appeared to clog the toilet, so she flushed it, ready to turn off the water valve at the first sign of trouble.

The water circled the bowl and whooshed away. Glad she avoided an emergency call, Willow returned into the room.

Dressed in a beige nightgown with brown spots on it, Nana swayed back and forth in her rocking chair, hugging a pack of toilet paper.

"Hey, Nana." Willow grazed her grandmother's sunken cheek with a light kiss. "Why the towel in the toilet?"

"I'm saving my toilet paper." Her grandmother wore disposable diapers, but from time to time, she insisted on using the toilet on her own. "The little girl steals my rolls."

The presence of a little girl, real or imaginary, mystified Willow. She visited her grandmother every other day and had never encountered a child within these walls. Nana had never mentioned the presence of one either. Until today.

I suppose this new tale isn't any weirder than a secret surgery room. "What little girl, Nana?"

Nana's gaze was locked on the window overlooking the parking lot. "She tiptoes bare foot in my bedroom while I sleep, and steals my toilet paper."

"Did you sleep this afternoon, Nana?" Had she known her grandmother battled intruders in her dreams, Willow wouldn't have suggested a nap. "Is that when you saw the little girl? Just before you woke up?"

Her grandmother's head snapped in her direction, and daggers flew out of her eyes. "I didn't dream her. She's the mean child with six toes."

The child's description, and her grandmother's animosity, threw another invisible punch into Willow's chest. Blaming the disease ravaging Nana's mind didn't ease the pain, and despite her best efforts, Willow couldn't repress the bittersweet emotions reverberating throughout her body.

"I cut my finger, Nana. I need to get to the hospital. I can't unclog another toilet tonight." *I suppose I should be grateful you didn't toss your diaper in the bowl and tried flushing it.* "You cannot throw towels in the toilet, okay? Just let the little girl play with the rolls. I'll bring more toilet paper tomorrow."

Her grandmother rested her chin on a roll. And groaned.

Throughout the day, nurses and patients alike walked into the examination rooms with food and beverages, feeding Zachary's body and replenishing his spirit.

"One of the nurses will call you in the next three days with the results of your blood test, Mrs. Whitmore. If there's any issue, she'll book you an appointment to come see me again next week." In normal times, Zachary agreed with the standard practice of only calling the patient if something abnormal showed up, but most of his patients felt the medical system had failed them. After being ignored or neglected for years, they deserved an extra dose of care.

Nurse Angela walked in while he updated Mrs. Whitmore's chart. "Would you mind seeing one last patient, Dr. Auckerman? It's a bleeding injury."

"Sure." He might as well since he suspected Nurse Angela would stay behind to take care of the patient's injury if he refused. "Let him, or her, in."

The head nurse handed him a sticky note with the name of the patient. Willow Mitchell. He entered it into his tablet and browsed her personal information. If the twenty-four years old woman had been born a day later, she would have shared his birthday.

16

Though a decade had elapsed since he was her age, Zachary felt the weight of these years more acutely than any others. He hadn't accomplished what his heart desired, and his life had taken a somewhat tragic and unexpected turn, forcing him to reconsider his path.

Nurse Angela ushered a young woman with short curly blonde hair inside the examination room. "This way, Mitch. Dr. Auckerman will take care of your hand. And if you give him the list of your grandmother's medications, he might even be able to look at it this week."

Stock-still beside a chair, his latest patient stared at him like a doe caught in the headlights of an eighteen-wheeler. A thick bandage blotched with blood was wrapped around her left hand.

"I'll go get a suture tray, in case you need it." Angela left the room and closed the door behind them.

"Hello, Willow, or do you prefer Mitch?" Zachary assumed that Mitch, the nickname used by Nurse Angela, was a derivative of Mitchell. Nonetheless, he always checked with his patients before calling them by any other names than the ones written in their charts. "I'm Dr. Auckerman. Would you like to sit?"

"You're a doctor?" The woman flopped on the chair, holding her injured hand. "A real doctor?"

Zachary rubbed his chin. The stubbles tickled his palm, reminding him how much the long day had taken its toll on his physical appearance. It didn't help that he didn't shave in the morning or that he wore a checkered shirt and a pair of worn-out jeans. Then again, he hadn't planned to treat patients. "I may not be dressed for the job, but I'm a licensed hospitalist trained in emergency medicine and pathology. I'm qualified to perform C-sections, remove appendixes, and treat injured hands."

Her expression morphed into something akin to astonishment. "I didn't mean to imply you were not qualified, Doc, or properly dressed. You look fine to me." A lovely rosy tinge blushed her cheeks. "I'm just astounded I missed the news of your arrival."

How she missed the news didn't puzzle him as much as how so many residents learned about it. "I arrived last night. May I look at your injury?"

"Sure, but now I feel bad for keeping you here this late on your first day." She sat on the swivel stool next to the examination bed then placed her hand on top of it. "I'm really sorry."

"I'm not." Regardless of the time of day or night, Zachary enjoyed interacting with his patients. "Can you tell me what happened?"

She scrunched up her nose. "I was cutting the rusty bolt of a toilet tank when the saw slipped off the groove. It nicked my finger and the side of my hand."

"You *nicked* it?" The blood on the bandage he was unwrapping suggested more than a nick. "Are you sure the finger is still attached to your hand?"

"Last time I checked it hadn't fallen off." Small chuckles coursed down her arm. "I actually wouldn't mind losing one, but not this one."

"You wouldn't?" He exposed the injury and counted one too many fingers, all fully developed. "I see..." In the majority of cases, extra fingers were either inherited or associated with a genetic condition or syndrome. "Was one of your parents born with extra digits? Any other health issues I should be aware of?"

"I'm healthy, and no one in my mother's family was born with any birth defects, but I'm also missing half my family tree. Maybe there are extra fingers growing on those branches." She shrugged. "I should have it amputated, it'd be easier to find gloves that fit, but I'm too busy to take time off."

"There's nothing wrong with your extra finger, but I get the issue with gloves." Most parents would have asked for the extra digit to be removed when their child was young, so Zachary couldn't help but wonder what prompted her mother's decision. "May I ask why your mother didn't consider surgery?"

"I guess it didn't bother her, or my grandmother, since it didn't impact *their* childhood." The emphasis spoke of youthful trials. "Can you fix my hand so I can use it? I have a hot water tank to replace tomorrow morning."

He knew nothing about changing water tanks, but it sounded like a busy morning. "I'll do my best. Can you bend your pinky finger?"

His patient grimaced curling and uncurling her six fingers. The blade had sliced her pinky sideways from the first knuckle up then lacerated the fatty part of her palm, but luckily for her, the injury hadn't compromised her mobility.

Once he ensured the laceration was clean and clear of any foreign materials, Zachary disinfected it. "When did the accident happen?"

"Two hours ago, maybe..." She appraised him with mystical amber eyes. "I know I should have come right away, but they only had one toilet. I couldn't leave them stranded, but I did bandage the wound and slip two sticky gloves on top to slow the bleeding and prevent infection while I fixed it. Getting all my fingers in was quite an exercise."

Her witty sense of humor tugged at a heartstring he thought he'd severed years ago. "You deserve a few credits for succeeding," he teased, peering at her other hand where he counted four fingers and a thumb. "What happened to your wrist?"

Her skin was red and irritated. "I used duct tape to seal the gloves."

"I see..." A knock on the door followed by the nurse's entrance stopped him from inquiring about Willow's work.

"Sorry it took so long. I had to answer the phone." Nurse Angela placed the tray on the examination table. "Suture or butterfly bandage?"

Since his patient didn't intend to take it easy, Zachary used stitches but only time would fully heal the wound.

As a precautionary measure, he also gave Willow a tetanus shot since her previous booster dated back six years, then wrapped a bandage around her hand. "Keep the wound clean, change the bandage regularly, continue wearing gloves, and stop by after work tomorrow so I can have another look at it."

Willow nodded. "Thank you, Doc."

Following his patient's departure, Angela raised an inquisitive brow. "If you keep telling them to come back, Doctor, you and I will sleep here every night, and my husband will leave me for another woman."

"Well, if we're to spend every night together, you better start calling me Zachary," he quipped, amused by her sense of humor. Nurses were doctors' best allies, and from what Zachary had witnessed today, the head nurse performed above and beyond the call of duty. "What happens if an emergency occurs at night?"

"On any given night, there's a nurse on duty and a security guard at the hospital. If help is needed, I get a call." A disarming smile floated across her lips. "Now *you* will get that night call. By the way, did Mitch show you her grandmother's list of medications?"

"No. I guess she forgot." *Or she didn't want to bother me.* Regardless, he should have remembered to ask.

"No worries. I'll remind both of you tomorrow. Now hurry up to finish your paperwork. You had a long first day." She gathered the suture kit. "Someone will come and clean the room after you're gone. Don't even think of touching anything. I'll see you in the morning, Doctor *Zachary*."

Laughter rose inside his chest. "Good night, *Angela*."

* * *

Zachary ventured into the wintery night. The snow had stopped falling, but the chilly wind biting his face had thrust the temperature downward. He hurried to sit behind the wheel of his SUV on a seat harder than a block of ice. To his relief, the engine started without complaining despite the minus twenty-one degrees Celsius indicated on his dashboard.

The seat warmed up while he drove around town in search of an open grocery store. Past a closed gas station, he stumbled on a street sign that rang a bell. If he recalled her chart correctly, Willow lived on that street.

Her house was dark, just like the gas station and grocery store. Resigned to the fact he wouldn't be able to fill his refrigerator tonight, he returned to the mobile home he rented behind the church.

Someone had shoveled his driveway and piled half a dozen grocery bags on the tiny front porch.

After his long shift, a warm sensation spread through Zachary's body. To be needed and appreciated felt amazing.

Chapter 2

Awoken at 5:30 a.m. by her alarm, Willow checked the weather app on her phone and shivered getting up. *It's going to be a crazy day.*

Every time the weather forecast called for an overnight temperature below minus twenty-two degrees Celsius, she set her alarm early so she could eat breakfast before she had to respond to her first emergency of the day. The lower the temperature, the busier she got in the morning. As a result, she avoided booking major projects before 10:00 a.m. in the winter. It allowed her to deal with emergencies without deviating too much from her schedule and disappointing too many clients.

She turned the radio on and brewed a fresh pot of coffee.

—chilling minus twenty-eight degrees Celsius with a wind chill of minus thirty-six this morning, folks. Make sure you bundle up your kids. So

far I haven't received any report the school isn't open, but it may change, so stay tuned.

The school never closed, regardless of the temperature, but that inconspicuous detail appeared to enter Artie Denzel's left ear and exit through his right without grazing his brain. It didn't matter how often the school principal tried to set the record straight, Denzel still fed false hope to children for breakfast.

In other news, Judge Douglass Drewer was nominated to fill a vacant seat at the Ontario Court of Appeal.

Drewer grew up in Ojibson. After obtaining his law degree in Toronto, he relocated to Ottawa where he worked as a criminal lawyer before moving up the ladder to judgeship. His new appointment will take effect on January 29th.

It is currently 5:45 a.m. and I'm your morning host Artie Den—

Willow's phone rang. The number on the screen belonged to a client who never winterized his lodge. "Why didn't I become a teacher?"

* * *

Following the 6:02 a.m. call that woke him up, Zachary rushed to the hospital.

Screams echoed in the corridor.

According to the nurse on duty, Susan was in intense labor, even though she'd shown no early sign of labor the previous day.

He turned a corner and came face to face with an older nurse in green scrubs. "I'm Dr. Zachary. Where's Susan?"

"Glad to see you, Doc." An aura of febrile apprehension surrounded the plump matron. "I'm Nurse Heather. Mom is in O. R. One with her husband. Baby is breech."

"Breech? When I examined her yesterday, baby was positioned with its head down." If baby was able to flip overnight, there was a chance Zachary could flip it back. "Any signs of distress?"

"Mom is three centimeters dilated, but baby is still high and doing good." Nurse Heather turned on her heels and headed toward Operating Room One alongside him. "It's her fourth child. She wants it out."

Trying to manipulate a baby involved risks, but so did performing a C-section. "How were her three previous deliveries?"

"She sneezed her boys out. Labor is a new experience for her." The nurse pushed the door open. "Susan, the doctor is here."

Framed on one side of the operation table by Angela, and the other by a weary father dressed in surgical gown, Susan squinted kneeling forward.

"Let's get you to lie down, Susan. Slowly..." Angela repositioned the mother-to-be with the help of the husband. "Keep breathing."

A guttural scream surged from Susan's throat and reverberated in the room. "That hurt... That really, really hurt."

Well... labor usually hurts. Still, the pain seemed excessive for this stage. "Let's see what baby is doing, Susan." Zachary felt her round belly, searching for the head and the bottom. "Get me the ultrasound machine."

Angela let go of Susan's hand to roll in the portable ultrasound machine.

His patient's belly rippled when Zachary applied the gel to her skin. "Baby doesn't like the cold." He flipped the screen toward Susan while moving the probe around her belly. "You may want to enroll this little one in gymnastic class. What you just felt was baby flipping again. See here?" Stilling the probe on the lower part of her abdomen, Zachary pointed at the screen. "That's baby's head. It's not engaged yet, but it's facing the exit. Now, we want gravity to keep pulling baby down. It would help if you could sit, kneel, pace the room, even walk up and down the corridor. The nurses will keep an eye on you and baby, so don't venture too far."

The emergency had turned into a normal delivery. Since his services were no longer required at this time, Zachary left the room and ventured into the staff lounge adjacent to the nurses' station.

Two security guards, a middle-aged man named Cain and a young redheaded woman, chatted near the counter where a machine dripped dark liquid into a pot. The invigorating smell of fresh coffee teased Zachary's nostrils.

"Coffee is almost ready, Doc." The woman raised an empty cup. "Would you like one?"

"Yes, please." Zachary had met Cain last night on his way out, but not the female guard. "Are you on day shift?"

"I came to relieve Cain. It's his sister in labor in there." Her expression mellowed. "Cain is too afraid to ask, so I will. How's Susan?"

Cain held his cup so tightly, his knuckles had turned white. "The boys need their mother. You're not going to let anything happen to Susan, right?"

"Baby is in the right position." Zachary bowed accepting the cup of coffee from the twenty-something woman. "Mom will pop him or her out sometime today."

A sigh of relief lifted the invisible weight slouching Cain's shoulders. "That's good.

Very good. Maybe you could make it a baby girl... to give Susan a break from three rambunctious boys."

In light of the flips and turns of the last few hours, this new baby may well prove more rambunctious than all its brothers together, regardless of its gender. "Sorry, Cain, but my success rate in the gender department is about fifty percent." Zachary's quip relieved the tension inside the lounge. "I'm getting off the subject here, but could one of you recommend a good plumber? I think my pipes froze overnight and I can't get a hold of my landlord."

The female guard, who still hadn't volunteered her name, checked her cell phone. "We have three plumbers in town, so it depends on what you want. Quick and cheap fixes, good repairs with sound advice, or outstanding work with lifetime warranty."

"Not sure I agree, Mandy." Cain took a sip of his cup. "Arnold added weird clauses to his lifetime warranty. He's not as outstanding as he used to be. Besides, he doesn't pick up after himself. My wife can't stand him."

"Yeah, you're right. I forgot how messy he can be." Mandy glanced back and forth between them while scrolling down her phone. "Would you like me to call them and check which one is available this morning?"

The offer brightened Zachary's day. "Please and thank you. And if you could book the good-repair, good-advice plumber, it would be greatly appreciated. I rent Chester's mobile home behind—"

Nurse Heather barged into the lounge. "Baby is crowning."

* * *

Willow hated to interrupt, but this morning every second counted. "I don't want the name of your important guy, Mandy. Just tell me if there are any young children in his house."

A childhood friend, Mandy worked as a security guard at the hospital. As such she should grasp the concept of priority. "No kids. He lives alone and he's at work."

The *important* guy had earned a spot at the bottom of Willow's list. "I should be able to get to him around noon."

"Noon?" Mandy sounded appalled. "But his pipes are frozen and—"

"Everybody's pipes are frozen." Willow answered emergency calls according to her own code of urgency. Homes with babies and toddlers first. Unoccupied houses last. She didn't care about her clients' occupation or bank account. The majority of them understood her priorities and appreciated that she cared about the most vulnerable. The ones that questioned her priorities were free to use Eugene's or Arnold's services. "I'll call you when I'm ready to head his way. Where does he live?"

A sigh of resignation coursed through the line. "Chester's trailer. I'll arrange for someone to unlock the door for you."

"Behind the church?" Willow could have sworn the last tenant had vacated the ice box weeks ago. "Tell your guy he has to pay me. I'm not billing Chester." The old coot still hadn't paid her for services rendered last spring. *No more credit for him.* Her phone beeped. "I have another call. Bye, Mandy."

Willow hung up, but before she accepted the other call, she glanced at the screen. It was the nursing home. Again.

Please, make it a plumbing problem. Please... "Hello?"

"Hi, Mitch, it's Elisabeth. I didn't wake you, did I?" The director never bothered with small talk when toilets overflowed or pipes burst. It could only mean a Nana problem. "Your grandmother is hallucinating a little girl who cut her finger. Do we have your permission to increase her meds?"

Another little girl? Really? Willow regretted mentioning her injury in front of her grandmother. "No, you don't have my permission. I'll get back to you tonight, I'm too busy right now."

* * *

31

Zachary took advantage of his lunch break to visit the patients' wing where Susan and her fourth child rested in a double room. Her husband sat on the second bed cradling his infant daughter while his wife slept.

Unwilling to disturb them, Zachary backtracked and bumped into the female guard. "Sorry, Mandy."

"I was looking for you, Doc." She smiled a heartwarming smile framed by deep dimples. "The plumber will be at your house in ten minutes. I'm sorry I couldn't get your pipes thawed any sooner, but there's no queue jumping, not even for a doctor. Would you like me to go unlock the door?"

He'd never expected special treatment because of his profession. Besides, nobody was home. It didn't matter when the plumber showed up to fix the pipes.

"Thank you, but the timing is perfect." Zachary lived five minutes away and his next patient wasn't scheduled to show up for another twenty-five minutes. "Going home gives me an excuse to enjoy a few breaths of fresh air."

The breaths of frozen air he took between the entrance of the hospital and his SUV chilled his upper airway. He didn't mind the cold, but from what he heard on the radio, the Arctic front that had settled over northern Ontario intended to overstay its welcome.

A white utility van was parked in front of his trailer and an individual bundled into a yellow hooded parka and carrying a toolbox knocked on Zachary's front door.

He pulled into his driveway then rushed outside. "I'm coming."

The individual spun around and the hood of his parka fell backward, unmasking the plumber's identity. "Doc?"

The look of surprise on her pretty face matched Zachary's.

"Willow?" He suddenly recalled their conversation from last night, and her occupation hit him. In retrospect, he should have clued in when she mentioned the toilet tank. *How did I miss that?* "Thank you for coming to my rescue."

She raised a brow. "You're my *important* client?"

Embarrassment threatened to redden his freezing cheeks. "Client, yes, but no more important than any of your other clients. I had a patient in labor, so Mandy offered to call. I apologize if she tried using my profession to get faster service."

"I never gave her a chance to give me your name—or your profession. You ended up at the bottom of my list the moment she said nobody was home." A mischievous smile blossomed on Willow's lips, wrinkling her eyes. "Are you going to let me in? It's your fair turn right now, but if it makes you feel better, I could push you further down my list."

"I like fair." Amused, he unlocked and invited her in. "How's your hand?"

"It's sore." She took off her boots. "I only had time to change the bandage once since I thawed my first pipe. I'm guessing my crazy day resembles yours at the hospital."

"Crazy sounds about right." Yesterday she'd mentioned a hot water tank during her visit, which was another clue he'd missed. "Have you replaced that water tank yet?"

The dubious look she served him answered that question. "I have three more clients after you, then I'll tackle the tank, assuming no other emergencies arise. So, which pipe froze? The one in the kitchen, in the bathroom, or both?"

"Kitchen only." It never occurred to him, until now, that shaving and enjoying a hot shower had been a luxury he almost missed this morning. "I shut off the main valve and turned all the faucets on to release the pressure."

"Good." She disappeared down the hallway. Moments later, pipes rattled in the walls and water rushed into the bathroom but nothing in the kitchen. Then silence filled the air.

The frozen water hadn't thawed, but it didn't sound like any pipes had burst. All in all, Zachary supposed it could be worse.

Willow entered the kitchen where she opened the cupboards beneath the sink. "The insulation in the walls is minimal. If Chester wasn't such a scrooge, he'd winterize his trailer properly, but since he's not the one living in it, he doesn't care." She pointed a flashlight at the space underneath the sink. "If you bend down, you'll see there's a vent on the back panel."

He knelt beside her. Her shoulder brushed his, prickling his skin. Confounded by the strange feelings she stirred up, Zachary forced his mind to focus on the cupboard. The light shone on a grill covering a large hole. Cold air escaped the opening.

"Who installed a vent there?" From his position, he couldn't see any dial or knob to close it.

"I did." She leaned the flashlight in a corner then retrieved a screwdriver from her toolbox and proceeded to unscrew the grill. "To stop the pipes from freezing you need to keep the cupboards open when the temperature drops below minus twenty."

"Good to know." The open doors allowed the ambient air to enter the vent and warm up the pipes, preventing them from freezing. *That makes sense.* "Why do I have a feeling my heating bill will cost me a bundle?"

"Because you're smart?" A sassy smile played on her lips. "Actually, it's not foolproof. Below minus thirty, you also need to let the water run in the kitchen sink, the bathroom sink, and the tub. And don't forget to open the cupboards in the bathroom as well."

The continuous flow would stop the water from freezing in the pipes, which meant he needed to pay particular attention to the weather if he worked all night or if he went on vacation. "What about the washer?"

The grill tumbled in the cupboard.

"Those pipes run in an indoor wall." She plugged in a heat gun, a tool he'd used in the past to remove paint, and she pointed it at the hole. "They've never caused any trouble, that I know of."

"That's not reassuring me." *No wonder Chester was so eager to sign the lease.*

* * *

In the doctor's place, Willow would move out, but since she didn't know the circumstances under which he'd chosen to rent that trailer, she kept her mouth shut. She doubted Chester had listed all the problems the previous tenants encountered. Coincidently, none of them had stayed more than seven months, but the doctor was an intelligent man. It shouldn't take him more than a few weeks to realize Chester had taken him for a ride. She predicted he would vacate the place before Easter.

Though she couldn't see the doctor, Willow felt his presence near the sink.

"There's water trickling, Willow." To hear him speak of droplets of water with the same soothing voice he used while tending to a patient alluded to a kind and caring personality. "Want me to go turn the main valve back on?"

Her heat gun set aside, she reached into the hole and felt the length of the two pipes. "Go ahead but be ready to turn it off if I yell *stop*."

She'd already dealt with one cracked pipe this morning. Another one and she might not be able to install that water tank until after supper. Water sputtered then splashed into the sink, but nothing on her fingers.

After waiting a few more seconds, she pulled her upper body from the cupboard, but kept the doors open. "We're good, Doc," she yelled.

By the time he returned with a first-aid kit tucked under his arm, she'd put away her tools and fetched one of her new business cards. Most of her clients paid her by electronic transfer, so she'd redesigned the back of her card. At the top, it read *Payment Due,* followed by an empty box. The line below said *Payment To Be Made To,* followed by her email address. She'd also added easy instructions on how to proceed with an e-transfer.

She wrote the amount he owed her in the empty box and presented him with the card. "Sorry, Doc, but if I bill Chester, I won't be paid until I'm old and cranky. You, on the other hand, can subtract that amount from your monthly rent."

Rich green eyes scrutinized her. "How much in unpaid bills does Chester owe you?"

"Roughly two hundred dollars." *Two hundred twenty-six dollars and fifty-one cents, but who's counting?* "Chester is the only client I've ever blacklisted, but what infuriates me the most is not the money he owes me but the fact he's one of my few clients who can afford to pay me right away— and the only one who chooses not to pay me at all." Venting felt good until she recognized how unprofessional she sounded. "I'm sorry. I was out of line."

"I'm bound by secrecy, remember?" The doctor took her bare hand into his and nudged her toward the kitchen table. "Have a seat, Willow. I want to look at your other hand."

His touch was soft and gentle, and she liked that he called her Willow, and not Mitch. When she dared look at him, he smiled. He'd tied his rebellious brown hair into a ponytail, and while a few strands had managed to escape, he looked respectable all clean-shaven. Not to mention ruggedly handsome.

Caught fantasizing about him, she silently admonished herself. The new doctor was in his thirties and single. Most of the eligible women in town, including all the pretty nurses working with him, had undoubtedly already set their sights on him.

No point kidding myself. A plumber with a shady lineage didn't stand a chance to attract a man like him. He was only interested in her injury. "Now? I have other clients to see, and you have patients waiting."

"I know, but when I was in med school, my mentor liked to remind me that I needed to take care of myself if I wanted to be able to take care of others." He pulled out a chair in a not-so-subtle invitation for her to sit. "I'm sure the same principle applies to plumbers."

Unable to counter his compelling argument, Willow removed her glove. While she didn't expect immediate improvement, she doubted her hand should look worse than yesterday, but somehow it did. She suspected the beginning of an infection.

The brow he raised reinforced her self-diagnosis. "You need antibiotics. As soon as I'm done cleaning it, I'll give you a few samples to start taking now until you can fill the prescription. Try changing the bandage between every client... or every other client. And I still want to see you at the hospital after you finish installing that water tank. Promise you'll meet me there tonight?"

It pained her to realize his excellent care might heal her hand but at the expense of her heart. "Okay..." *To keep seeing him isn't a good idea, but what choice do I have? He's the only doctor in town.* "I promise, but I may be late."

"Late is good. It'll give me time to review that list you haven't provided me yet of your

39

grandmother's medications." He winked at her, awaking the pathetic butterflies that had been hibernating in her heart since Willow lost her husband. "Tell me more about your granny."

Pooping hell, Willow, keep it professional and stop fantasizing about him. She took a deep breath and exhaled a long sigh. "Well... Nana is..." *Crazy* sounded rude. "Nana is a handful."

As she tried not to flinch under his tender ministrations, Willow filled him in on her grandmother's health issues and behavior.

* * *

Alone in Exam Room Three, Zachary reviewed Rose Mitchell's medications and the changes proposed by the director of the nursing home.

I'm glad you didn't give your permission to implement these changes, Willow. Some of these medications could have serious side-effects. Zachary couldn't recommend implementing any changes until he performed a full exam on her grandmother.

Curious to know who suggested these new drugs, and hoping the director didn't take it upon herself to evaluate the health of her residents, Zachary looked on both side of the sheet of paper for a name.

A note was scribbled on the back of the sheet. *Recommended by Nurse Wiedrich.*

The name didn't ring a bell. Whoever that nurse was, his or her name wasn't on the hospital roster.

Hoping to shed a light on Nurse Wiedrich's identity and credential, Zachary headed for the nurses' station.

The station was deserted.

On the wall behind the computer, a bronze plaque commemorated the construction of the hospital twenty-one years ago. Zachary disliked imagining the kind of medical services the local residents received prior to its opening. With these grim thoughts in mind, he found Angela sipping on a cup in the staff lounge.

The steam rising above the rim of the hot beverage caressed her lips. "Doctor Zachary? What are you still doing here?"

"Playing catch-up." *And waiting for Willow.* "What can you tell me about Nurse Wiedrich?"

Angela rolled her eyes lowering her cup. "Let's just say he could probably kill a cadaver. Why?"

Zachary hiccupped a chuckle. *Incompetent* would have sufficed. "His recommendations regarding Rose Mitchell leave something to be desired."

"I expected that much." An edge had crept into Angela's voice. "Want me to book

41

Rose for an appointment so you can determine her condition for yourself?"

"Yes, please." In light of Wiedrich's reputation, Zachary would look into the feasibility of visiting all the patients of the nursing home in the next few weeks. "How well do you know Rose?"

In such a small town, everybody knew everybody, no matter how old or young.

"Too well." A grimace contorted her face. "She could have used a heart."

A heart? No heart medications were listed, but some of the other drugs could be detrimental to a patient suffering from heart issues if administered in high dosages. "What's wrong with her heart?"

"Nothing in the ticking department, but it could have contained more love. It wasn't easy for Mitch to grow up with six fingers. She was one smart girl, sharper than a scalpel." Angela drummed well-manicured fingers on her cup. "Some kids at school teased her mercilessly. Dr. Holloway tried to convince her grandmother to let him remove her extra digit, but Rose refused. I overheard her once calling Mitch her meal ticket. I wish I could unhear her comment."

And yet, despite her childhood, Willow grew up into a compassionate woman. Zachary's admiration for the spirited plumber reached a new high, for which he chastised himself. In order to avoid conflicts of interest, or any other kind of conflicts, certain boundaries existed between a doctor and his patients. He hadn't settled in yet and he already questioned where that blurry line between duty and feelings stood in a town of only one doctor. "Do you know when the grandmother began showing signs of instability?"

"Her mind started slipping away during Mitch's long absence, but no one noticed she'd *rescued* two dozen stray cats and dogs until Mitch returned five years ago. You should have seen the mess." The look of dismay on Angela's face spoke volumes. "The house was deemed uninhabitable. Most nineteen-year-olds wouldn't have stayed to clean up, or obtain guardianship of an elderly lady, but Mitch did. She cared for Rose until she had to move her into the nursing home."

These new revelations didn't help in curbing his enchantment for Willow. "You mentioned a long absence. Where did Willow go?"

"She eloped with a guy when she was sixteen. Where she lived during those three years, or when or how her husband died are—" Steps resonated on the tile floor, and Angela stretched her neck toward the open door.

Nurse Camille paused in the doorway. "A resident of the nursing home has died, Doc. The director requests your presence."

Chapter 3

The director of the nursing home didn't strike Zachary as the chatty, friendly type.

Aside from providing her name, Elisabeth Brown had skipped small talk and hadn't invited him to sit. Her expression looked as clinical and dispassionate as her office.

"This is the death certificate, Doctor." Elisabeth handed him a sheet of paper on which someone had listed *Heart Attack* as the cause of Alphonse Morrison's death. "Since you're the only physician in town at this moment, the honor of signing the document falls on you."

Declaring a person dead and signing a death certificate didn't belong in the same category. While many could attest to the first, only a few could sign the second.

"Who concluded he died of heart failure?" If the director believed Zachary would blindly accept her conclusion, she faced a rude awakening.

"Nurse Darius Wiedrich." The name coming out of her mouth didn't inspire any confidence. "He's been treating Alphonse for the last six months ago. Darius is very conscientious, and I trust his judgment."

Considering Darius's reputation, Zachary was stunned to hear Elisabeth holding him in such high esteem. *Maybe you shouldn't.*

She presented him with a pen. "If you could please sign at the bottom?"

Unfortunately for her, her insistence didn't match Zachary's tenacity. "Has the next of kin been notified of Mr. Morrison's passing?"

"Of course." The director leaned back in the chair she occupied behind her desk, but annoyance had crept in her voice. "I called his daughter Meg, Meg Grosbeak, ninety minutes ago. She was shocked, naturally, but she took comfort knowing we would arrange the transfer of his body to the funeral home."

Among the patients that Zachary had examined at the hospital this morning was a sixty-something woman by the name of Meg Grosbeak who suffered from high blood pressure. Monitoring her condition was part of his duty as her attendant physician. No one should take offense if he visited her to inquire about her health, pay his respects—and ask her permission to examine her deceased father.

"I will sign the certificate once I review Mr. Morrison's chart." *And hopefully examine his body.* "Is the deceased still in his room?"

"No. An attendant from the funeral home picked him up an hour ago." Elisabeth stared at him with cloudy eyes. "In all fairness, Doctor, shouldn't you spend your time taking care of the living instead of delaying the cremation of a ninety-one-year-old man whose heart stopped ticking? I was under the impression you had enough patients to keep you busy for the next few years."

Zachary believed the dead deserved as much respect as the living, a notion she might not comprehend. Besides, suspicious vibrations had sizzled through his body at the mention of Alphonse's upcoming cremation. Elisabeth Brown sounded too eager to burn any evidence contrary to Nurse Wiedrich's conclusions.

"I'll keep your advice in mind, Mrs. Brown. In the meantime, I expect a copy of Mr. Morrison's complete file, personal and medical, on my desk at the hospital by midnight. Have a good evening."

* * *

Knowing every death upset her grandmother, whether the victim had been a mere acquaintance or a long-time friend, Willow drove to the nursing home following her visit to the hospital.

46

From what she'd gathered talking to Nurse Angela, Willow had missed Dr. Auckerman by a few minutes, but he'd looked into Nana's meds and wanted to examine her. His course of action pleased Willow but learning about the death of another resident had put a damper on the good news.

Fourth death in a month. What are the odds?

Granted, the average age of the residents revolved around ninety years old, but the three previous deaths had involved able-bodied residents living on the second floor. These residents shouldn't have expired without warning.

Nurse Angela hadn't provided the name of the latest victim, so Willow counted on Nana to give her more details.

"Nana? Who am I kidding?" According to her grandmother, a woman was strangled by the ghost of her husband, another woman was hit by a snowmobile, and a man fell overboard and drowned. "Nana's imagination shows no boundaries or ties to reality."

As Willow parked in a visitor's stall of the nursing home, she glimpsed the doctor's light blue-green SUV leaving the parking lot. *I guess I missed him again...*

Bottling up her disconcerting disappointment, Willow walked into the old building. In the entryway, a numeric keypad was affixed to the wall, but it hadn't functioned in years, or so she learned from her grandmother's neighbor, a gentleman named Alphonse. Anyone could enter or leave without being monitored or seen.

The lobby was deserted, Elisabeth's office door was closed, and the lights in the narrow corridor were dimmed. How two wheelchairs could cross each other without colliding was a mystery Willow had no intention of solving tonight.

She didn't encounter a soul on her way to her grandmother's bedroom on the second floor, but she heard wailing and moaning coming from behind a few closed doors.

No wonder Nana is hallucinating ghosts. The building should have been demolished then reconstructed instead of being converted and refurbished. Disheartened by the way Elisabeth managed the place, Willow knocked on her grandmother's door and waited.

When no one answered, she used her key to unlock. "Nana? It's Willow. Are you up?"

A light shone in the room. Her grandmother sat motionless in her rocking chair, holding on to a cup with both hands.

Saddened to see Nana wear the same nightgown as yesterday, Willow pried the empty cup from the bony fingers curved with arthritis. A smidge of liquid pooled at the bottom of the cup. She brought it to her nose and sniffed. "Rum?"

"I'm not crazy. I'm not old." The chair creaked. "And I'm not drunk."

Startled by the sudden exclamation, Willow placed the cup on the night table. "Who gave you rum, Nana?"

Nana rocked back and forth, staring at the ceiling. "The drug dealer."

"Who?" *When did you start hallucinating about a drug dealer?*

"He stabbed Alphonse." A lone tear snaked down the ridges of Nana's withered face. "I want to go to bed."

Surprised to hear Alphonse's name, Willow gripped both armrests to stop the chair from rocking, then knelt in front of her grandmother. "Did something happen to your neighbor Alphonse? Is he the person who died tonight?"

"Alphonse always gave me his brownie at supper." Her grandmother pouted. "I want brownies."

A forlorn sigh died in Willow's chest. "First, let's get you into a nice warm bath."

Nana disliked taking a bath, but when she didn't argue, Willow entered the bathroom to run the water.

The tub was full of toilet paper rolls.

* * *

The clerk at the funeral home didn't bat an eye when, instead of a death certificate,

Zachary presented him with a letter signed by Meg Grosbeak giving him permission to perform her father's autopsy.

"Mrs. Brown will be displeased not to be able to embalm the deceased before she visits her brother, Judge Drewer, to celebrate his upcoming appointment to the Court of Appeal. The judge grew up here, you know." The clerk, a large man in his sixties, spoke with enthusiasm. "I'm sure you've heard of him. Everyone in town knows him or knows of him."

"Kind of." Zachary had overheard his patients talk about Drewer's appointment. The judge's reputation reached far and wide and blended in every shade of gray. Zachary had also heard the name Brown, which rang a discordant tune. "Your Mrs. Brown, is she related to Elisabeth Brown, the director of the nursing home?"

"Same woman. The funeral home belonged to her late husband. After he died in a fire, I was afraid she would sell, but she learned the ropes and kept running it. In any case, I believe Meg is right to want to know about her father's death, even if it means delaying the funeral. I've been dealing with corpses for over forty years. Not much fazes me. That's the reason folks around here call me Henry the 8th, though I prefer when they don't add a number after my name. It's not like I'm killing anyone. I always make sure they're dead cold when they get here, not just cold. I know Mrs. Brown trusts Nurse

Wiedrich, but you can never be too careful. Mr. Morrison's body is down here." With a broad sweep of his arm, Henry gestured for Zachary to follow him down a staircase. "Will you perform the autopsy in the embalming room, or should I bring the body to the hospital?"

The hospital morgue, located next to the lab in the east wing, contained half a dozen refrigerated bays where bodies could be stored, two stainless-steel tables on which to perform the autopsies, and all the instruments needed for the procedures.

"Hospital." Zachary didn't want anyone breathing down his neck.

"As you wish."

The clerk led Zachary into a large embalming room where the body of an elderly man lay naked on a stainless-steel table.

Irked to see no one had protected his dignity in death, Zachary draped a sheet over him, stopping at Alphonse's shoulder, then brushed a thin and damp strand of white hair off his temple. Puzzled, he bent over the deceased. A faint woodland scent tickled his nose. "Who washed him?" Any evidence the skin could have retained had been lost forever, heightening Zachary's suspicion. "Who undressed him? And where are his clothes?"

"He was naked in bed when I picked him up from the nursing home." A frown creased Henry's oily forehead. "Come to think of it, he was kinda wet, as if he'd just stepped out of the shower but hadn't dried himself thoroughly."

From his pocket, Zachary pulled out a pen and a prescription pad on which to scribble notes. "Did you see a towel anywhere in the room? What was his position in the bed? Was he under the sheets? Was—"

"Hold on, Doc." The clerk raised his hands taking a step back. "I don't usually do pickups. That's Marshall's job, but he went to visit his sick mother. I wanted to take pictures of the deceased, but Mrs. Brown told me it wasn't necessary. Mr. Morrison was lying on his back with his head on the pillow and both arms over a thick blue and red comforter. It covered his torso up to his armpits. His eyes were closed. He looked so peaceful I could have sworn he was sleeping. I checked twice to make certain he was indeed dead. As far as I recall, the drawers of the dresser were closed, but the doors of the closet were open. I didn't see any towels, clothes, or pajamas on or around the bed, or on the floor, but I didn't go into the bathroom. I loaded the deceased on a gurney, brought him here, and laid him on the table, as instructed by Mrs. Brown."

Impressed by Henry's memory, Zachary noted every detail.

Steps resonated on the staircase, growing louder by the second and culminating with the arrival of Elisabeth Brown.

"Good evening, gentlemen." Her sharp gaze sliced Zachary like a razor—at the carotid. "I heard you convinced Meg to perform an unnecessary autopsy on her father. You just couldn't let dear Alphonse rest in peace, could you?"

"Only doing my job, Mrs. Brown." *And listening to my gut instincts.* Getting the uncanny feeling he'd overextended his welcome, Zachary turned toward the clerk. "Please have Mr. Morrison transported to the hospital in the next fifteen minutes. I'll await his arrival."

Zachary walked out of the funeral home before anyone could object.

On his way to the hospital, he stopped by his mobile home to open all the cupboards in case the autopsy dragged late into the night. A red note stuck out of the rusty black mailbox affixed next to the front door. He pulled it out.

Unimpressed to be reminded to pay his rent on time, Zachary shoved the note into his pocket and entered. A mouse scurried over the kitchen counter before disappearing behind the refrigerator.

Less than impressed by the presence of an unwelcome guest for which Zachary didn't intend to pay rent, he called his landlord. On the fourth ring, he reached Chester's voicemail.

Zachary's frustration grew another notch. He hung up wishing he'd met Willow before renting this trailer.

* * *

Nana's snoring provided a background noise while Willow removed her grandmother's dirty clothes from the closet and stuffed them into a large garbage bag.

An attendant was supposed to attend to Nana's daily hygiene, help her dress and undress, take her to the dining room, clean her bedroom and bathroom, change her sheets, and do her laundry.

Finding out no one had bothered sending her clothes to the laundry made Willow question how often the other tasks, for which she paid good money, were performed. "No wonder you're often in your nightgown. You have nothing clean to wear."

She vowed to wash them overnight and bring them back before breakfast. Too many imaginary people visited her grandmother at night. Willow didn't want Nana to call in the morning to complain about someone stealing her clothes.

Nana's new walker was relegated to the end of the closet. She didn't like the built-in seat, and therefore, refused to use it. Willow was tempted to make the old walker standing beside the bed disappear, but it wasn't a battle worth waging tonight.

An antique cuckoo clock hung above the dresser. The birdie no longer peeked from its nest to sing, but the arrow-shaped hands continued to keep the time. *Midnight.*

"It's time I go home."

After giving the closet one last look, Willow turned its light off, and froze. A small circle of light shone on a black dress that no longer fit her grandmother. Willow slid the dress along the rod, exposing the side wall. At shoulder height, a ray of light filtered through a ragged hole the size of a quarter.

Puzzled, she bent over the walker, and resting one knee on the seat, she peeped through the hole with one eye. At the sight of a blue and red comforter, a gasp died in Willow's throat. *Nana? Are you peeping at your neighbor?*

The bed was unmade and the light in the bedroom was on, but no one was home.

Alphonse's bedroom is on that side... isn't it? As the identity of the absent neighbor sank in, her grandmother's words came back to bite Willow. *The drug dealer stabbed Alphonse.*

The tears in Nana's eyes had been real. Alphonse's death had affected her, and while it wasn't inconceivable her grandmother had cared about him, it was also possible Nana had witnessed something disturbing through that hole.

If someone stabbed Alphonse to death earlier this evening, the staff may not have had time to thoroughly clean the bedroom yet. Searching Alphonse's bedroom was a bad idea, but Willow couldn't ignore the feeling that something fishy was going on. For her Nana's sake and hers, Willow needed to find out if her grandmother's rambling contained any elements of truth.

Willow stepped out of the room, walked down the deserted corridor, and knocked on Alphonse's door.

When no one answered, she tested the doorknob. It wasn't locked. She hurried in and turned to lock it behind herself only to realize no deadbolt or latch were mounted on the inside. The thought that anyone could come in and out without the knowledge of the resident didn't reassure her.

All the lights were on.

The layout of Alphonse's bedroom was different than her grandmother's. His room contained a double bed decked with a beautiful iron headboard, and a wooden dresser with picture frames and knickknacks on top, and appeared larger.

At first sight, Willow didn't see any signs of struggle or traces of blood.

Both closet doors were pushed to the left. Far and few between, shirts and pants were draped over or folded onto white hangers, and a pair of blue slippers with holes at the toes were neatly aligned against the side wall.

56

On the back wall, between a blue shirt and a pair of jeans, Willow spied a hole.

To be able to see into Alphonse's room had been sheer luck. Had his shirt or jeans hung slightly to the right or the left, or had someone slid the closet door back, Willow wouldn't have seen his bedroom from Nana's closet.

Whoever made the hole couldn't have intended to peep into the next bedroom, or else they would have looked for a better location. Convinced that someone had inadvertently punched that hole, Willow turned her attention to the bed. Underneath it, dust bunnies played hide-and-seek with a sock and a red—

"What do you think you're doing?"

Startled, Willow jumped to her feet.

Hands on her hips, the director scrutinized her from the doorway.

"Elisabeth? I..." *Think, Willow. Think.* "I was looking for Nana's slippers. Green slippers." Her grandmother didn't own any green slippers, but green was the first color that popped into Willow's mind. "She can't find them, and I thought... Nana mentioned Alphonse often and—"

A lopsided smile softened Elisabeth's stern expression. "No need to feel ashamed, Mitch. It's healthy for seniors to be active at night, but Alphonse was usually the one hopping in her bed, not the other way around."

Willow's jaw dropped. *Nana has a sex life, and I don't?* Something was wrong with that picture, not that she wanted to picture her grandmother in bed with Alphonse, or any other men. "I... I didn't know that..."

"That I knew? Most keys unlock most doors, so sometimes we have to intervene when our residents are too loud, or when a third person wants to join in." Elisabeth gestured for Willow to leave Alphonse's room. "It's late, Mitch. Go home. If I find your grandmother's green slippers, I promise to return them to her."

Bed-hopping? And threesomes? Stunned, Willow staggered outside. Serious health issues were associated with risky sexual behavior. *Nana needs a full physical exam as soon as possible.*

* * *

In the solitude of the morgue, Zachary's fatigue faded away. He preferred treating live patients, but on occasion he enjoyed giving a voice to the dead.

The discovery of the puncture mark at the back of Alphonse's neck energized him. "Did something bite you or did someone inject you with something?"

At this time of year and in this weather, Zachary could count on one hand the number of species capable of biting or sucking on anyone. The absence of any other marks anywhere else on the body ruled out most of the usual suspects—bed bugs, lice, mites, and fleas—which left Zachary with two likely culprits. A spider and a needle.

"Well, Alphonse, that's not a spider bite." The neck wasn't a common injection site, but the puncture mark could only have been made by a needle.

According to Nurse Wiedrich, Alphonse had died of a heart attack, but many drugs could induce a heart attack in healthy individuals. A toxicology test would detect the presence of most of them in the victim's bloodstream with the notable exception of potassium chloride. The drug was used to treat patients with low levels of potassium. An overdose would cause severe arrhythmias and mimic a heart attack. The patient would die within minutes of the injection and the large amounts of potassium released in the bloodstream during the heart attack would mask the presence of the drug.

The lab technician at the hospital only processed routine tests. Any other tests needed to be couriered to an accredited lab, which didn't deter Zachary. "I'm requesting a full tox screen, Alphonse, but between you and me, it may not reveal anything incriminating."

Seeking unequivocal answers, Zachary pried the thoracic cage open, revealing among other organs, the victim's heart and healthy lungs.

The door of the morgue swung open.

"Elisabeth finally sent his medical file." Nurse Camille waved loose sheets of paper toward the deceased. "May I look at the body?"

"Sure." With a bloody glove, Zachary invited her to stand on the opposite side of the stainless-steel table. "Tell me what you see."

"Lungs are clean, but the heart suffered a major blow." Her nose twitched in the most adorable fashion. "I know he was ninety-one, but he ran his yearly half-marathon last spring and jogged every morning around town regardless of the weather. I guess it proves anyone can suddenly drop dead."

"What does his nursing home medical file say?" Zachary had checked the hospital records. The deceased hadn't visited the premises since Dr. Holloway gave him a full physical four years ago. At the time, the tests hadn't reported anything wrong or suspicious.

"Let's see..." She frowned flipping through the pages. "The only thing they monitored was his blood pressure, which fluctuated between normal and slightly elevated. Nothing else. According to this, no lab tests, routine or otherwise, were done since Alphonse moved into the nursing home three and a half years ago. In Darius's place, I'd keep a closer look on the residents under my care." Frustration peeked through the words. "I can't believe Elisabeth chose him over me."

Her short outburst mystified Zachary. "Did you apply for his job?"

"I kind of did. I'd just moved back home. There was an opening at the nursing home. Full-time, decent pay and benefits, and no nightshift..." Nurse Camille hugged the chart to her chest. "Don't take me wrong, Doc, I love working here and I came to enjoy nightshifts, but at the time, the other position looked more appealing."

Unlike Darius, Nurse Camille hadn't given Zachary any reasons to question her qualifications or dedication. "Did Elisabeth say why she favored Darius over you?"

"Nope, but my mom thinks Darius is... how shall I put it... Elisabeth's latest toy boy." The nurse rocked on her heels. "After her husband died, Elisabeth acquired the reputation of being somewhat of a cougar, not that it matters why she hired Darius. I wouldn't dream of working anywhere else, especially now that we have you here. It's nice to work with the same doctor every day. Anyway..." A rosy shade blushed her cheeks. "I'll leave the chart on the counter in case you need it. Is there anything else you would like me to do for you?"

Since she grew up in town and looked to be around the same age as Willow, Zachary risked a personal question. "Would you know how Willow Mitchell's husband died?

If I could gather some details, it may prevent me from accidentally saying something inconsiderate the next time I see her."

"Well, from what I heard, he died under suspicious circumstances." His nurse stared at him with an unreadable expression. "Back then, some rumors suggested that... that Mitch might have been involved. To be honest with you, I don't know where the truth lies, but in your place, I'd probably avoid mentioning him at all."

The rumors only increased Zachary's curiosity. "Thank you, Nurse Camille. That will be all."

Chapter 4

It took a moment for Willow to realize her phone, and not her alarm, was ringing. Through heavy eyelids, she squinted at the screen. *4:57 a.m. Area code 613. Unknown caller.*

The origin of the call rang a silent bell in her sleepy mind. Thinking it could only be an emergency since no one in their right mind would disturb someone this early in the morning, she answered. "Hello…"

"Good morning, Lo." The soft ghostly voice from the past instantly awoke Willow. "It's been a long time."

"My name isn't Lo, it's Willow." The sobriquet tore at the stitches keeping the invisible wound in her heart closed. "And it's not morning yet, Brigitte. What do you want?"

After a lifetime of neglect, Willow couldn't care less if she offended the woman who birthed her. The term mother didn't apply to Brigitte. Unlike Nana who'd stayed in touch with Brigitte, Willow hadn't spoken to her in eight years.

"In case you forgot, I'm still your mother. I have the right to call whenever it pleases me." The dismissive response proved Brigitte hadn't changed one iota. "Do you have any idea how much money he'll pay for your finger?"

An unhealthy dose of aggravation built inside Willow's chest. She could only imagine the crazy tale that her grandmother had spun about the injury that Willow had sustained fixing the toilet. It had undoubtedly lit up dollar signs in front of Brigitte's eyes.

"I don't want to hear about another one of your get-rich-quick schemes." Willow didn't intend to sue anyone. Granted her hand became infected, but she bore the responsibility of the accident—and anything else in her life—alone. "Go back playing with your married men, or better yet, get back here and take care of Nana."

"You're such an ungrateful child, Lo. Some days I wonder why I bother with you."

The line went dead. Brigitte had hung up without saying goodbye.

"What was that about, Brigitte? Were you high?" It wouldn't surprise Willow to learn her mother had become addicted to something. "That would certainly fit your lifestyle."

Something bigger than a nasty cut to her finger had to have been at play to warrant that not-so-good good morning call, but Willow had no desire to be dragged into

64

Brigitte's world of intrigue and dirty secrets. Getting married at sixteen had taught Willow a lesson she wished she'd learned before exchanging any vows. *Desperation doesn't excuse bad decisions.*

Since the call had chased away her sleep and dampened her mood, Willow checked her phone. Unlike real phone calls, messages didn't always wake her up. If someone needed her help now, she would be more than willing to accommodate.

Three new messages waited in her inbox.

The first came from Mrs. Blake, a charming widow who lived in a small house with too many cats, all of which hated Willow. It was sent at 3:09 a.m.

> *My toilet is clogged. Please come whenever you have a chance.*

Willow suspected Mrs. Blake of having thrown a few too many fur balls in the bowl again, but regardless of what caused the problem, a clogged toilet qualified as an emergency. Had Mrs. Blake phoned instead of texting her, Willow would have gone right away. *You're first on my list, Mrs. Blake.*

The second message further darkened her mood. No point deluding herself into thinking good news could originate from the nursing home at 4:22 a.m.

Mitch, we found your grandmother trapped in the service elevator around 4 am. Come see me in my office between 4 - 5 pm. We need to talk. Elisabeth.

First her mother, then her grandmother. Life conspired against Willow, but considering Nana's escapade, she agreed with Elisabeth. They needed to talk.

The third message consisted of a notification. A client had sent her money.

Willow clicked on it and couldn't help but smile. The doctor had paid her, but then she did a double take at the amount, and her jaw dropped. This wasn't the amount she'd charged him. He'd overpaid her by two hundred dollars.

Their discussion flooded back into her mind, hitting her like a rogue wave. *I can't accept, Doc.* It wasn't that she didn't appreciate the gesture, but he wasn't responsible for Chester's debt. A note was attached to the payment.

I was rudely reminded last night to pay my rent on time, so I followed your advice. I deducted the cost of yesterday's repairs, and the money Chester owes you, from the amount I transferred to him. Rest assured I didn't

66

mean to step on your toes, but I couldn't resist the opportunity to right two wrongs with one click.

Please accept my help in the spirit it was given. Zachary

With a simple note, the doctor had restored her faith in humanity. *Not the doctor. Zachary.* Willow couldn't believe he used his given name. The man behaved like the doctors in her dreamy novels.

"Well, *Zachary*, Chester is bound to be fit when he sees your transfer is short by two hundred dollars." Being paid was nice, but she owed Zachary a huge thank you for also brightening her day.

Enough dawdling. She needed to get to Mrs. Blake's house before the dear elderly lady forgot she shouldn't use the toilet, and it overflowed.

* * *

A knock on the closed door ended Zachary's power nap in Exam Room Three.

After his short night, he'd indulged in a few fifteen-minute naps throughout the day to stay sharp and focused. The smallest examination room, conveniently located in a nook and away from the noise, offered privacy. In the weeks to come, Zachary planned on transforming it into his personal office since he didn't use it to examine patients.

Re-energized, he rolled down his sleeves and tucked his shirt back into his pants. "Come."

"Dr. Auckerman?" The hospital lab tech, a tall brunette with French braids hugging both sides of her head, stepped in and presented him a report. "These are the results of Mr. Morrison's tests." The name *Mary* was written in green ink on the breast pocket of her lab coat underneath the drawing of a turtle. "If you need me to run other tests, I'll be in the lab for another hour or so."

"Thank you, Mary."

Zachary flipped through the report. All the results were within acceptable parameters.

His earlier autopsy confirmed Mr. Morrison had died of a heart attack. The elderly man had suffered from mild coronary artery disease for which he wouldn't have shown any symptoms. Heart blockage in the twenty-five percent range rarely caused restriction to the blood flow, and there weren't any indications these mild blockages had contributed to his death.

Disappointed, Zachary tossed the report in the counter.

"Doctor Zachary?" Angela peeked around the doorframe. "You have four patients left. Whenever you're ready for the next one, he's waiting in Exam Room Two."

For a second, Zachary debated getting a coffee first, but then it looked like he might get home at a decent time this evening. He didn't want to ruin his date with his bed.

* * *

Outraged didn't begin to describe how Willow felt when she stormed into the hospital. She needed someone to vent to before she exploded and caused too much collateral damage. On second thought, she should have triggered the detonation in Elisabeth's office. *That woman—*

"Hello, Mitch. Is everything all right?" In the middle of the corridor, Nurse Angela scrutinized her from head to toe with a compassionate expression. "You look ready to pick a fight with a mama polar bear."

"I'm..." Willow was wound up tighter than a boa suffocating its next meal. "I want to move into an igloo on an iceberg, and I don't want anyone to rescue me."

"I hear you, girl." The head nurse patted her on the shoulder. "This afternoon we had a patient who came in drunk with self-inflected stab wounds. When he learned the doctor wouldn't see him right way, he stripped down naked in the middle of the crowded waiting room and began dancing on a gurney."

A ludicrous picture emerged in Willow's mind, tickling her throat. "You're kidding, right?"

"I wish." The head nurse rolled her eyes. "People were shrieking in horror, gasping in disbelief, or laughing hysterically, but then the guy fell off the gurney and passed out with his bloody junk in full display on the floor. After the mess I had to clean up, I'm ready to go home—and never come back."

The tale, too far-fetched not to be true, didn't alter Willow's feelings toward Elisabeth, but it curbed her deadly intentions. "My hand looks better. If you're too busy, I can—" A scream echoed in the corridor, startling Willow. "What was that?"

"The stabber stripper. He's sobering up in the drunk room." Nurse Angela sighed glancing down the corridor. "With my luck he'll start throwing up before my shift ends. Have a seat, I'll tell the doctor you're here. He's been waiting for you."

A few minutes later, Zachary appeared. He looked tired, but when he set eyes on her, a smile crept up his face, illuminating his eyes and dispelling his weariness. "Hello, Willow."

His reaction awoke the silly butterflies hibernating in Willow's stomach. *Stop fluttering around.* There was no way the mere sight of her had triggered such a transformation in him.

Sober men didn't give an ordinary girl like her a second look when she walked down a street unless they possessed ulterior motives. Between her mother's reputation and a few bad choices, Willow couldn't expect to attract a man like the doctor. However, she didn't doubt he was happy to see her. After all, she was his last patient. Zachary was probably eager to cross her off his list, go home, and relax after a long day.

Dejected, Willow followed him into one of the examination rooms.

* * *

Unsure how to interpret the myriad of expressions that crossed Willow's face, and afraid one of them might be related to his interference, Zachary braced himself for a confrontation.

The woman possessed two traits that he both admired and dreaded. A fiery nature and an indomitable character.

"If you're mad at me for the two hundred dollars, feel free to chew my head off." His head nurse had warned him about Willow's disposition when she arrived. "But then I would also like you to give me the opportunity to explain."

A timid smile tugged at Willow's lips. She extended her arm on the examination bed and presented her hand with her palm up, not curled into a fist. "I would be lynched if I decapitated the only doctor in town."

Her reply released a fit of laughter from his belly. "Fair. Does that mean you're not mad at me?"

Amber eyes observed him. "It wasn't your battle, but you already know that, so why did you help me? Chester won't take too kindly to your extortion scheme."

Honesty was another refreshing quality that Zachary admired in people, though he wouldn't go as far as calling his scheme extortion. "I'm trying to rattle Chester's chains."

Willow raised an inquisitive brow. "What did he do, or didn't do, this time? Or am I too nosy?"

Until they got to know him better, women tended to treat Zachary as a doctor first and a human being second. Willow's no-nonsense behavior defied the norms, norms that meant nothing to him. The man underneath the scrubs felt at ease in her presence, and for reasons he didn't want to fathom, Zachary trusted her.

"I had an unwelcome visitor last night, the furry kind from the rodent family." Before signing the lease, Zachary had inquired about pest problems, but the landlord had assured him in writing that he wasn't aware of any problems. "I tried contacting Chester, but he's not answering, so I paid my rent, minus what he owes both of us."

"That'll get his attention." She flinched when he probed her injury. "May I ask if it was a mouse or a squirrel? I saw droppings of both under the trailer when I was fixing a leak last spring. I can even tell you where the point of entry is."

Thanking his lucky stars, Zachary gazed at her in wonder. "It was a mouse. Does Chester know about the droppings?"

"Of course he does. I warned him he should seal the crack before they squeeze through and infest the trailer. I even offered to solve the problem for thirty bucks since I was already working in the crawl space." She grumbled some unsavory terms and colorful adjectives under her breath to describe the sleazy landlord. "Had he not owed me money at the time, I would have done it for free. I even took pictures to send him—and to protect myself in case he accused me of causing the damage—and you know what he said? *Go ahead and fix it, but I'm not paying you a cent more.* Yeah, well, he didn't pay me a cent of what he was supposed to pay me either."

Willow's temper was flaring, reminding Zachary of his own reaction last night. *Chester doesn't bring the best out in his contractors or tenants.* Had Zachary stood in her boots, he would also have recorded the damage. Then it hit him. If he could prove his landlord lied about the pest problems, Zachary might be able to break the lease. "Do you still have the pictures?"

"Of course I do. I wasn't planning to delete them until the day I die." She pulled out her phone from the back pocket of her jeans with her free hand. "They're also in my *sent* folder, which proves he knows. That should help you renegotiate your monthly rent."

"I'm aiming to move out if I can break the lease without paying the equivalent of six-months-rent penalty." The clause with the swift penalty should have raised a red flag, but desperate to find a place to stay before he arrived in town, Zachary had signed the lease without looking at the trailer first.

"Six months? That's steep." A grimace contorted her face into a mystified expression. "If you want these pictures, I'll need your email or phone number."

As he provided both, it occurred to Zachary that he would soon run out of professional excuses to see her. The realization exposed the void he hadn't bothered filling since he caught his girlfriend cheating on him. Then again, he wouldn't qualify his new schedule as relationship friendly either.

"Feel free to contact me anytime, Willow." The words came out of his mouth of their own accord before he could recall them. *For goodness' sake, Zachary, she's your patient.*

"Actually..." The woman playing havoc with his mind gazed at him with keen interest, and he found himself holding his breath. "I have a favor to ask you, a big favor, but I don't want it to be an imposition."

His curiosity unleashed, he patted the hand he'd finished treating then reluctantly let it go. "I promise to do the best I can, so what's the problem?"

"Nurse Angela told me you looked at my grandmother's meds and you think she might need a full exam..." Willow expelled a shaky breath. "Any chance it could be sooner rather than later?"

From what she'd already told him about her grandmother, Zachary took the request seriously. Besides, Willow didn't strike him as the type of woman who made a habit of begging for favors or crying wolf. "Has something else happened to your grandmother since we last spoke?"

* * *

Willow didn't mean to dump it all on the doctor. However, once she started telling him about Nana, she couldn't stop, but she managed to contain her fury when she recounted that Elisabeth instructed Darius to sedate Nana after finding her in the service elevator.

The doctor bolted from his stool. "I'll get a blood collection tray, then we'll go see your grandmother at the nursing home. Just give me a few minutes."

As his words sank in, Willow gasped in disbelief. "Now?"

With his fingers wrapped around the doorknob, Zachary looked at her over his shoulder. His five o'clock shadow accentuated his enigmatic expression. "Since we don't know what *Nurse* Darius injected her with, don't you agree it might be wiser to check on your grandmother sooner rather than later?"

His proposition surprised Willow, but in a weird way, it reassured her that the doctor didn't seem to trust Darius any more than she did. "Are you sure it's not an imposition?"

"I'm sure." The ghost of a smile brushed his lips. "Come to think of it, why don't you follow me. That way we can exit through the east wing."

Too stunned to argue, Willow tailed him into a lab where he picked up a kit, then into a lounge where Camille brewed a pot of coffee.

The pretty nurse with dark exotic features eyed Willow with unconcealed interest. "Is there anything I can help you with, Doc?" A sexy French-Canadian accent rolled off her tongue.

"I'm making a house call at the nursing home." Zachary grabbed a gray winter coat from a standing coat rack. "Call me if there's an emergency."

Without waiting for an acknowledgement, he grazed the small of Willow's back with his hand in what could only be interpreted as an invitation to accompany him.

"If you don't mind, Willow, I'd like you to drive with me." He led her toward his SUV. Parked at the opposite end of the parking lot, the vehicle was sprinkled with snow. "That way we can talk on the way back."

That sounded like a valid reason, and though she would have preferred a different one, Willow couldn't refuse the offer.

* * *

Troubled by the events that Willow had recounted in his SUV, Zachary followed her into her grandmother's room. *If there's any smidgen of truth behind Rose's intimate relationship with Alphonse or her stabbing allegations, I'll need to reassess her health issues and Alphonse's death.*

Willow turned on the ceiling light. Her grandmother lay motionless in bed, eyes closed, undisturbed by their presence.

Without knowing which drugs were administered to her, or how much, Zachary dreaded the possibility she might have lapsed into a coma.

"Nana?" Visibly worried, Willow sat on the bed and stroked her grandmother's shriveled face. "Nana, wake up. It's Willow."

Her grandmother's eyelids fluttered. "Brigitte?" The name that Rose whispered through thin lips created a palpable strain between grandmother and granddaughter.

None of the people that Zachary had encountered since moving to Ojibson sported that name. His curiosity was piqued, but he didn't intend to solve the mystery of Brigitte's enigmatic identity until after the tension in the room dissipated.

"It's Willow, Nana. You didn't need to tell Brigitte about my hand." Willow withdrew to the edge of the mattress. "The doctor came to examine you."

Zachary moved from the foot of the bed to the other side. "I'm Dr. Zachary, Rose. How are you feeling?"

"Babies cry in the basement." Tears pooled in her eyes. "Bad surgery."

It didn't sound like Willow had exaggerated her grandmother's condition, and though Willow hadn't mentioned any babies, Zachary was intrigued by the elderly lady's obsession with secret surgeries in the basement.

"I'll check on the babies this evening, but first I need to examine you." When Rose didn't object, he performed a physical exam then drew some blood. "I heard you and Alphonse were good friends, Rose. Can you tell me what happened to him?"

"He was stabbed." Her eyes rolled at the back of her head. "He's dead."

"Where was he stabbed? On his chest?" The eyebrow that Willow raised didn't deter Zachary from inquiring further. "On his leg?"

"In his bedroom." The elderly lady identified the location at the other end of the peephole that Willow had mentioned, not the site of the wound, but then Rose touched the nape of her head. "The drug dealer stabbed him."

This was the same location where Zachary had discovered the puncture mark. *Plunging a syringe in someone's neck could be misinterpreted as stabbing.* Unfortunately, due to her failing mental capacities, Rose couldn't be considered a reliable witness. "Who was the drug dealer, Rose? Did you see him?"

"They had gray hair." Her gaze locked on the ceiling, Rose squirmed in bed. "They took the babies."

"Easy, Nana." Willow stroked her grandmother's arm while looking at him. "You're not thinking a grayish man might be involved in Alphonse's death, are you?"

Afraid the walls might not only have eyes but also ears, Zachary refrained from acquiescing. "I'm simply trying to determine the extent of her delusion."

The dubious look that Willow served him spoke of her incredulity, but he was pleased when she didn't argue any further.

Later he would ask her to describe Darius and the nursing home attendants.

Before they left, Zachary also needed a urine sample. "Can you go in the bathroom and pee in a cup for me, Rose? Or do you need your granddaughter to help you?"

"Don't want to pee." The elderly lady gripped the sheet and bunched it against her bony chest. "It hurts."

The discomfort heightened Zachary's concerns. He presented a sterile cup and three gloves to Willow. "Your grandmother may have an infection. Make sure you wear two gloves over your bandaged hand."

Willow moaned snatching the gloves and container. "Come on, Nana. Time to pee."

* * *

If becoming a nurse had ever appealed to Willow, helping someone pee in a cup would have changed her mind. She would rather deal with clogged toilets than temperamental bladders.

"Time to sleep, Nana." While she put her grandmother back to bed, Zachary rummaged through the closet.

Once her grandmother dozed off, Willow focused her attention on the doctor bent over Nana's new walker. His right knee resting on the seat, he held on to the handles while peeping through the secret hole.

From Willow's viewpoint, it almost looked like he knelt on a stepladder and peeked from the last rung.

More of Nana's words came back to haunt Willow. *I saw him at the top of the ladder*. The notion that her grandmother had really glimpsed something that she shouldn't have didn't sound as farfetched as it once did.

Unsure if someone stood within hearing distance from Alphonse's closet, Willow cleared her throat, but stopped short of asking Zachary if he saw anything interesting.

"I could only get Nana to pee half an inch." The dark liquid inside the cup that Willow had placed in his tray didn't look healthy. "Will that be enough?"

He moved away from the closet and retrieved his tray from the night table. "That's sufficient. Until I review the results of the tests, I do not recommend changing any of her medications."

Elisabeth won't be pleased. Not that Willow cared. She trusted the doctor, and though many more questions swirled in her mind, she waited until they sat in his SUV to probe further.

The heated passenger seat warmed up her bottom within seconds of him turning on the engine. She regretted not paying the extra money for that option when she bought her van. "Doc, do you believe there's a smidgen of truth in Nana's ramblings?"

"First, I would really like it if someone in town would just call me Zachary before I lose my identity." He glanced at her with a lopsided smile. "Second, what I'm about to tell you *must* stay between us."

Mystified by his requests, Willow stared into the night. If she didn't know any better, she might think he flirted with her, and if he knew her any better, he might not trust her. *This is hopeless.* "In this case, my lips are sealed, *Zachary.*"

"When I performed Alphonse's autopsy, I discovered a small puncture mark on his neck where your grandmother claimed he was stabbed." The dashboard didn't emit enough light to distinguish his expression, but he sounded concerned. "It's possible she witnessed something innocuous, something unrelated to his death, and imagined the worst."

"But you're also thinking it's possible that drug dealer may not be a figment of Nana's imagination, and that he injected Alphonse with something that killed him, aren't you?" Then suddenly, the other deaths resurfaced in Willow's mind. "Could that be why four residents, all of them in good shape, died in that many weeks?"

The SUV came to an abrupt stop on the side of the deserted road.

Zachary snapped his head in her direction. A flickering lamppost cast shadows on his face. "Alphonse is the fourth to die in a month?"

Captive of his fiery gaze, she nodded, but the feeling she might have opened a can of worms feasted on her insides. "Two women and two men. All above eighty years old."

"In all fairness, these four residents in their autumn years may have suffered from underlying conditions that precipitated their deaths. The timing may be coincidental." He drummed his gloved fingers on the steering wheel. "On the other hand, the source of any delusion often stems from a drop of truth. Who's Brigitte? And where does she fit in the picture?"

Willow couldn't stifle her heavy sigh. "Brigitte is my mother, and I use the term loosely. She was Nana's only child. She dumped me on Nana's lap after I was born, and she's been stepping in and out of my life ever since." *Mostly out.* Willow broke eye contact with him. "Nana told her about my injured hand and now Brigitte thinks she can sue someone over it and make a few quick bucks." Most days, Willow wished she'd been abandoned on the steps of a church or at the door of a fire station so she could have been adopted by a family who wanted her. "Brigitte doesn't fit in any picture."

"I get it, and for what it's worth I'm really sorry." As a doctor, Zachary would have encountered his unfair share of dysfunctional families, many far worse than hers. "I don't think your grandmother is intentionally mixing up your names, Willow, but her delusion about a drug dealer and secret surgeries may explain her presence in the service elevator. Is there a chance you could come up with a believable story that would allow us to inspect the basement? A follow-up call? A maintenance visit?"

Pleased by his use of the pronoun *us*, Willow racked her brain for an excuse to visit the basement of the nursing home. "I fixed the boiler back in September. Since we're experiencing a cold snap, it wouldn't be a bad idea to check it again and make sure it's working properly. I should be able to squeeze in a visit in the next few days, assuming I'm not inundated with emergencies. When would it be more convenient for you? Early morning? Evening? Weekends?"

"I would prefer evenings." He patted her good hand. Twice. "Any evening that I'm not inundated with too many emergencies."

"Don't worry, Zachary. I won't go snooping without you." Though it raised the possibility they might discover something amiss or disturbing, this clandestine outing gave her a chance to spend time with him outside the hospital.

Chapter 5

The test results from the accredited lab arrived late Friday afternoon, but Zachary didn't get a chance to look at them until after he sent his last patient home. At the end, his timing didn't matter. The results didn't reveal anything abnormal or suspicious.

The puncture mark still stumped him, but since he couldn't prove it was related to Alphonse Morrison's death, Zachary signed the death certificate. *That's it, Alphonse. I'm releasing your body. May you rest in peace.*

Zachary then turned his attention to Rose's results. Willow's grandmother suffered from a urinary tract infection. In elderly patients, the infection could cause changes in behavior or delirium, and if left untreated, could lead to kidney failure or sepsis.

Disheartened, he leaned back in his chair. *Rose's symptoms should have sounded alarm bells in the ears of a qualified nurse.* The undiagnosed infection didn't only cast a black eye on the care provided at the nursing home but also further doubts on Darius's competence.

Because of these results, Zachary needed to prescribe antibiotics, change some of Rose's medications, and adjust others. He shuddered to think what would have happened if Willow had followed Elisabeth's advice. Darius's recommendations would have undoubtedly incapacitated the poor old lady in some way, shape, or form. *I hope that's not how you recruit more clients for your funeral home, Elisabeth.*

Zachary hadn't heard from Willow since they visited her grandmother on Wednesday evening. The temperature had dropped below minus thirty-five degrees Celsius the last two nights, so he could only imagine how many pipes demanded her attention. It wouldn't surprise him to learn she'd worked past midnight and hadn't had time to set up their clandestine visit to the basement yet. Under these conditions, he couldn't blame her for crawling into bed instead of visiting the hospital.

Still, he hoped to see her tonight. It had been forty-eight hours since he last talked to her, and it scared him to realize how much he missed her.

For the hundredth time, Zachary Auckerman, Willow Mitchell is your patient. Becoming infatuated with a patient was never a good idea, but he was the only doctor in town. Every resident was his patient.

Zachary couldn't even call her to his rescue. Against the odds, he didn't experience any water problems, but he also overheated his trailer, and left all the cupboards open and taps running. It was so hot he slept naked under a thin cotton sheet.

He also hadn't heard from Chester who appeared to be avoiding him, but Zachary had received a notification from his bank that his landlord had accepted his payment.

This situation is getting ridiculous. If Willow showed up tonight, Zachary would ask her opinion on Chester's behavior and other rental places while he examined her hand.

The door of his office burst open and banged against the wall, dislodging the sign glued at eye level. The silver plate with the words *Exam Room #3* written in black clunked onto the floor.

Elisabeth Brown kicked the sign under a cart, marring the rounded toe box of her black leather boot. The scratch created an optical illusion, making her right boot look smaller than her left one. "Where is my dead body?"

The bodies in her funeral home wouldn't feel offended by her discourteous attitude, but Zachary shuddered at the thought she might greet the residents of her nursing home in a similar manner. "Mrs. Brown, to what do I owe the pleasure of this *impromptu* visit?"

She crossed her arms over her fur coat, making no attempts to conceal her aggravation. "I came back early from Toronto so I could ready Mr. Morrison for his wake tomorrow afternoon only to find out you hadn't returned him yet."

When Meg Morrison agreed to let Zachary perform her father's autopsy, she'd told him that she wouldn't schedule the funeral until next week.

Zachary hadn't been apprised of any changes. "I was under the impression the wake wouldn't start until Monday."

Elisabeth pursed her lips as if he'd confessed to a monstrosity. "In these parts of the woods, *Doctor*, some mourners can only travel during the weekend. A wake must include a Saturday and a Sunday to give everyone a chance to pay their respects. Delaying Alphonse's wake by a week would only add to the family's grief and sorrow. Is that what you want?"

The thought that Elisabeth might have bullied Alphonse's daughter into accepting this argument crossed Zachary's mind, but since it hadn't prevented him from finishing the autopsy, he refrained from commenting.

The death certificate rested on the corner of his desk. He presented it to her. "I'll let the nurse on duty know you'll send someone to pick up Mr. Morrison this evening. Next time, please knock."

* * *

Willow's bank account didn't complain about the inflow of money associated with the cold weather, but her body might if that cold snap lasted any longer. She wouldn't be able to sustain working fifteen hours a day more than a few additional days.

Last night she'd lain down on the couch for a few minutes while her supper defrosted in the microwave only to wake up famished three hours later. By the time she finished eating, it had been too late to go to the hospital.

Afraid she might fall asleep again and miss seeing Zachary if she sat anywhere, she waited by the oven for her pizza to cook. She didn't want her supper to burn any more than she wished for the only roof over her head to go up in smoke, regardless of the pitiful memories buried within its walls.

While she ate, she reviewed the messages on her phone. Between two clients this morning, she'd texted Elisabeth to ask if the boiler functioned properly during the bitter nights and to let her know she could probably make a courtesy inspection if there were any concerns.

Willow had rewritten the text four times before sending it. On one hand, she hadn't wanted to appear too eager to go back in the basement, but on the other, wanted to make it appealing for Elisabeth to accept her offer.

Eight hours later, Willow was still waiting for an answer.

The response came as she readied to leave for the hospital.

> *The boiler is making loud noises. I would appreciate a free inspection tomorrow (Saturday) between 9 am and noon. Thank you.*

While she was pleased Elisabeth had taken the bait, Willow didn't like the reference to loud noises—or the feeling she'd been summoned to fix something for free. The boiler hadn't reached half its lifespan yet. She shouldn't encounter important—

The doorbell rang, putting an end to her pondering.

Willow opened the door only to freeze with her hand on the doorknob.

A RCMP officer stood on the porch. "I'm Constable Melanie Laforge. May I speak with Willow Mitchell, please?"

"I'm... I'm Willow." As much as Willow racked her brain, she didn't remember breaking the law since she moved back to Ojibson. "What can I do for you, Officer?"

A dimple was embedded in Laforge's left cheek, giving her a lopsided expression. "May I come in?"

Willow stretched her neck and glanced over the officer's shoulder. A RCMP cruiser was parked behind her van, blocking her exit. Constable Laforge's visit didn't reassure Willow since the closest RCMP detachment was located more than eighty kilometers west of Ojibson. No officer would have driven for over an hour unless a serious matter was at stake.

Her heart pounding against her ribcage, Willow invited her visitor in. "What is it about?"

The constable followed her into the living room. "It's about Brigitte Mitchell. You share the same last name. Is she a relative of yours?"

"She's my mother. Estranged mother." Willow's apprehension morphed into aggravation. *If it's bail money you came to collect, you knocked on the wrong door.* "What has she done this time?"

* * *

On his way out, Zachary stopped by the nurses' station manned by Nurse Camille for the night. She wore the same colorful Snow White and the Seven Dwarfs scrubs as the day he first met her.

"Are you going home, *Doc*?" The young nurse possessed the remarkable ability to brighten any patients' darkest day, and on her lips, the nickname *Doc* took a playful connotation.

"I'm debating leaving." Willow's no-show triggered an uneasy feeling in the pit of his stomach.

Nurse Camille leaned her elbows on the counter separating them. "I'll try not to disturb you with emergency calls tonight, but if I do, can I make it up to you?" Her eyes twinkled merrily. "There's a local country band playing at the Antlers Pub every Saturday night. I could buy you a beer since you're off-duty this weekend."

Despite his caseload, Angela had strongly suggested he took Sunday off. When he argued against it, she rescheduled the few patients she'd booked for Saturday and threatened to cancel his Monday appointments as well if he didn't enjoy the entire weekend. Zachary had swallowed the rest of his objections before his head nurse forced three days off on him.

"Never hesitate to call me, Nurse Camille. Dealing with emergencies is part of my job." Being a doctor wasn't a task, but on his days off he needed to be Zachary, the man under the scrubs. As such he'd never dated a female colleague or staff member, and he didn't intend to start this weekend no matter how beautiful that woman might be. "Please don't feel you owe me anything. Besides, I'm afraid I'm a rather boring guy. I wouldn't want to ruin your Saturday night."

The twinkles in her eyes abated. "Actually, Doc, spending the evening in a noisy, smelly, and crowded Pub wasn't my idea of fun, but when I heard Angela say you needed to relax, I felt compelled to show you some northern hospitality. She can be quite a mother hen sometimes, but I'm kinda glad you refused. Popcorn and movie night is a Saturday ritual in my parents' house, and I don't like missing it, unless I'm working of course."

"I completely understand, and I appreciate your honesty." The brief uncomfortable moment between them seemed to have vanished, hopefully without causing any ill feelings. "The funeral home will send someone to pick up Alphonse Morrison's body this evening. I already gave the paperwork to Mrs. Brown."

A frown creased Nurse Camille's forehead. "I bumped into her after she left your office. She looked ready to throw a lit match in a gas tank. What happened?"

"Who knows?" The entire meeting in his office, from Elisabeth's entrance to her departure, had struck a discordant chord. "Maybe she didn't enjoy the party in her brother's honor—or found it awkward to talk with living people under the age of eighty."

Laughter rose from Nurse Camille's mouth. "Go home, Doc."

"I will, as soon as I check on Willow Mitchell." He hadn't planned on stopping by her place. Until now. The lack of communication between his head and his heart threw him for a loop. An enchanted loop. "Good night, Nurse Camille."

* * *

The incessant ringing of the doorbell pierced the layers of confusion choking Willow's brain.

Outside the living room window, the lamppost across the street illuminated the mountain of snow covering the front yard. In its shadow on the left, she spied the tail of a vehicle in her driveway, and on the right, a strange silhouette standing on the porch.

She hadn't lowered the blinds yet. Whoever kept ringing the doorbell would have seen her curled on the couch. Since her unwelcome visitor showed no sign of leaving, she forced herself to get up.

Emotionally drained, she trudged to the vestibule, and dodging her boots she yanked the door open, ready to slam it as soon as she finished admonishing the visitor.

"I don't—" His presence on her porch late at night confounded her. "Zachary?"

"I'm glad you remember my name." The doctor smiled, a warm and comforting smile that washed away the years from his face, giving him the appearance of a teenager. "May I come in?"

"Why not? It feels like an open house tonight." She invited him into the living room and while he took his boots and coat off, she pulled the blinds down to avoid feeding the neighbors' curiosity.

The tick tock clock sitting on the mantle of the wood fireplace chimed ten times. Cold ashes filled the hearth. Had she known she would spend the evening at home, she would have started a fire.

"Willow?" Zachary touched her shoulder, startling her, then trailed his hand off her arm, leaving behind the illusion of a caress. "Did something happen?"

Assailed by conflicting emotions ranging from anger to something strangely akin to sorrow, and everything in between, she sat at the edge of the couch hugging her chest in search of heat and comfort.

"A RCMP officer came earlier…" Willow recalled their eerie conversation but not how long the constable stayed or when she left. "Brigitte died shortly after she called me on Wednesday morning. I don't know why it's affecting me. I was just an inconvenience she dumped on my grandmother's lap. It's not like I meant anything to her."

The cushion beside her caved in.

"Maybe, but she meant something to the young child you once were." Zachary draped an arm over her quivering shoulders, and she leaned into him. "Tell me about your mother."

Swayed by the huskiness of his voice, Willow traveled down memory lane, one uneasy back step at a time.

"I remember her long blonde hair and dark blue eyes looking down at me. She was beautiful, glamorous, and mesmerizing. Men wanted her, but only the ones with money could afford her. She enticed rich married men, first as a seductive mistress, then as a ruthless blackmailer. After squeezing her lover's wallet dry, she dumped him and sought new prey. Her reputation preceded her, but men couldn't resist her." Her mother had been nothing more than a high-end prostitute and scam artist, a humiliating truth that stained Willow's childhood. "When I was eleven, she bought this house for my grandmother with *their* money." Unlike Nana, Willow never liked the house. Now that her grandmother lived in the nursing home, she toyed with the idea of selling it and moving into something smaller and cozier. "I wasn't the only one aware of my mother's lifestyle, the other children at school were too. Sometimes kids can be crueler than adults, and it only takes a few to make one's life miserable." The derogatory names had rolled off Willow's back—after poking her skin and stinging her heart. "It wasn't bad enough that I was born with six fingers or that my mother didn't want me to have surgery, she loved staring at my hand with that grotesque smile on her *perfect* face and taking pictures of me." Had Brigitte possessed an ounce of decency, she would have given up her daughter for adoption. "Why couldn't she have abandoned me on the side of a road instead of forcing my grandmother to raise me?" The gentle strokes that Zachary bestowed on her back encouraged her to continue. "When I was fifteen, I overheard a phone conversation between Nana and Brigitte. I hadn't seen her in a few years. It hurt me to realize they'd stayed in touch but never bothered to include me. My grandmother was appalled that a man stopped paying my mother and dared threatening her. I was disgusted... and ashamed."

"Is that why you ran away at sixteen?" He murmured softly in her ear. "To escape your mother's past?"

A heavy sigh expanded her chest, churning up the painful truth. If Zachary knew she left town at sixteen, then he would also have learned of the circumstances under which she'd returned.

"I was a waitress at the Antlers Pub. Brett was... he was a wannabe country singer from North Bay. We hooked up backstage when his band performed at the Pub. Then one night, when we were both drunk, he asked me to marry him. I convinced myself I was in love with him, but you're right... I just wanted to escape Ojibson." She'd run but couldn't hide from her fate, a bittersweet fate neither better nor worse than the one she'd tried to escape. "We lived in his parents' basement in North Bay for three years. His father was a plumber and his mother worked at the local credit union. They were the parents I never had. They encouraged me to attend the local college, even paid for my tuition, so I followed in his father's footsteps. What I didn't learn in class, I learned from his father. His mom was the one who taught me how to cook, take care of finances, and run a house." To this day Willow still missed her late husband's parents. "Brett was two years older than me, but when I started making money and taking responsibility for my actions, he began to resent me. To paraphrase him, *I was no fun anymore,* so he hooked up with an ex-girlfriend who was engaged to an architect and got her pregnant." The moment Willow heard the rumors about the baby, she knew her marriage was over, not because of his infidelity, but because she couldn't care less who he slept with as long as it wasn't with her. "Brett's father was furious, the girlfriend's father was enraged, so to settle the situation, they all went hunting together." Mixing guns and bad feelings hadn't sounded like a good idea, and though the men proved her right, Willow didn't feel any satisfaction. Only sorrow and regrets. "They found Brett in a pond beside a dead moose. He'd left the camp alone at dawn with his rifle after a night of heavy drinking, shot the moose, then passed out face down in the water—or so both fathers recounted. The autopsy confirmed he was drunk, and he drowned."

"It was deemed an accident?" The intonation in his voice suggested a question, not an observation. "Do you believe the fathers' version of the events?"

When Brett's father urged her to go back to Ojibson after the funeral—and never come back—Willow accepted that the truth had died in the woods with Brett.

"My beliefs won't change the past." She met the doctor's gaze. "I'll remain a widow and a baby will still grow up without a father."

"You're right. That was a stupid question." A myriad of emotions swirled in his eyes, and she was at a loss to isolate one, but to her surprise, she didn't glimpse any pity, disapproval, or disappointment. "Why did you move back here and not start fresh somewhere else?"

Willow withdrew to the corner of the couch, and with her knees hugging her chest, she observed him. Zachary seemed to care, but then he was a doctor. Doctors were trained to show kindness and compassion, and from everything she'd witnessed, Zachary was an excellent doctor. It was foolish to entertain the idea he treated her differently than he did any other patients. Besides, after learning the details of her pathetic life, any feelings she might imagine he harbored had certainly vanished.

"Before moving anywhere else, I needed to find my bearings, to come to terms with my past, so I took my maiden name back and came home." She'd feared Nana would slam the door in her face. Instead, her grandmother had hugged her, a warm and fierce hug, the only one that Willow ever recalled receiving from her. "To be honest, I didn't intend to stay, but Nana's health had deteriorated, the house was a total mess... I guess I felt it was my duty to take care of her."

"I'm glad you stayed, or I wouldn't have met you." He leaned back stretching his arms over the top of the couch. "And I'd be freezing to death in Chester's trailer."

The dash of humor he added to the conversation dispersed some of the dark clouds hovering over her head. "Don't tell me your pipes froze again?"

"As much as I would like to call you to my rescue, I've been heeding your advice." With his fingers, he toyed with the fringe of the throw draped over the back of the sofa. "Did the constable say how your mother died or why it took her two days to notify you?"

Willow replayed the details in her mind, trying to make sense of them. "Brigitte phoned me around five on Wednesday morning then her maid found her dead three hours later. Stab wound to the chest. There was a pair of scissors in her hand. If Brigitte hadn't pulled them out, she might not have bled to death... I didn't even know she lived in a condo in Ottawa." The last Willow had heard, her mother lived in Toronto. "I don't know if the police managed to unlock her phone or if they had to request a transcript of her calls, but that's how they tracked me down. I was the last person she talked to, so the constable who was dispatched to give me the news wanted to know why Brigitte called me. I recounted our short conservation then told Constable Laforge every sordid detail I know about Brigitte. The only thing I couldn't provide was the names of all the men who had motives to silence her... They found prints on the scissors, trace DNA under her fingernails, and signs she struggled with her assailant. They can't tell if the assailant broke in or if Brigitte let him in, but the condo was ransacked."

"Scissors are weapons of opportunity." Zachary squinted at something above her head. "Whoever killed her may not have intended to do so. When you talked to Brigitte early that morning, did you have the impression she might be hiding something or be afraid of someone?"

"She was always hiding something, but she didn't sound threatened." Still, the timing of her mother's death within a few hours of their call unsettled Willow. "If anything, Brigitte sounded almost giddy, not that what she said made any sense."

"Would you mind telling me exactly what she said?" Zachary's interest in the call mirrored the constable's.

"She phoned at 4:57 a.m. to ask if I knew how much money he would pay for my finger. I wasn't interested in her money schemes. I cut my finger fixing a toilet. It was my fault. Why would I sue anyone? I told her to go back to her married men or come here to take care of Nana. She called me an ungrateful daughter. Her last words before she hung up were *I wonder why I bother with you.*" In retrospect Willow regretted answering the call. "Well, I wonder the same thing."

Zachary heaved a long sigh. "You could have seriously injured your hand with that saw, but I fail to grasp how your mother learned about it or how she intended to transform your injury into a money tree, unless..."

Constable Laforge had emitted the same objection, but without the *unless*, and Willow had agreed. "Unless what, Zachary? Brigitte phones Nana from time to time. She probably talked to Nana during one of her few lucid moments and learned I cut my finger."

"Maybe, but could she have meant your sixth finger instead? What do you know about your biological father?"

In the dead of the night, when sleep evaded her, Willow sometimes wondered about the man who shared her DNA, the man who betrayed his wife for a romp with her mother.

"I don't know the names of any of the wealthy fools my mother slept with before separating them from their money." *My father would have been rich, possibly blond, but he wouldn't have had blue eyes.* That much Willow had deduced since she wouldn't have weird coppery eyes if both her parents' eyes had been blue. "If Brigitte knew which man got her pregnant, she took his name to her grave."

"You inherited your extra finger from one of your parents. One of them would also have been born with an extra digit. It may not have been fully formed, and it could have been removed at birth, but one of them was born with a little stump on its hand or foot." He gently cupped her cheek, coaxing her to tilt her head in his direction. "It's a dominant trait, Willow. You may not necessarily pass it to *your* child, but if a child has it, then one of her parents *has* to have it. Are you sure your mother was born with only ten fingers and toes?"

She gazed into his eyes, the two darkening green orbs pulling her into their midst. Suddenly aware of his proximity, his manly scent, his warmth, she drifted toward him. Blurry words floated between them, peeling the hazy layers of her brain and sinking in one syllable at a time. Her mother never went out in public without a perfect manicure and pedicure. Neither her hands nor her feet sported any scars suggesting a previous surgery.

"I'm pretty sure it wasn't my mother—" Understanding struck her like a physical blow. She recoiled against the couch, and Zachary's hand dropped onto his lap, releasing her from his spell. "You're not suggesting my mother used my extra finger to blackmail my birth father, are you?" Arguing with him distracted her mind from the realization she'd almost kissed him, but it didn't prevent a tiny seed of doubt from taking root. "It's been twenty-four years, Zachary."

"Didn't you tell me your mother took pictures of your extra finger and refused to consent to its amputation?" The doctor used her own words against her. "Maybe your father left her before she realized she was pregnant. Maybe she wanted to use your finger as leverage in the unlikely event he would reenter her life. Or yours."

Fueled by Zachary's farfetched allegations and memories of the past, the wheels in Willow's brain spun at a dizzying speed. Could she have misinterpreted her last conversation with her mother? Could her extra finger have been some sort of insurance policy her mother tried to cash in long after it expired?

"Whichever finger Brigitte meant, it doesn't mean her extortion scheme is related to her death." Still, the argument sounded hallow to Willow's ears. "That would be a big coincidence, wouldn't it?"

Zachary winced. "I'm afraid I don't believe in coincidence. Could your grandmother know your father's identity? Could she have kept his name a secret all these years?"

As a child, Willow was sent to her room without breakfast, lunch, or supper— whichever meal came next—every time she dared ask Nana about her father. The punishment didn't curb Willow's curiosity, but it tied her tongue. The years had blurred her recollection of these events, making it impossible for her to speculate on her grandmother's intentions. Had disapproval, shame, or something else, prevented Nana from mentioning his name, Willow couldn't hazard a guess. Not even a wild one.

"Nana calls me Brigitte." Willow didn't trust her grandmother to blurt out the right name even if she recalled the man who got Brigitte's pregnant. "I fear whatever is left of her sanity will suffer a fatal blow once I tell her that Brigitte was killed. Do you think I should make a special trip to the nursing home this evening or wait until tomorrow when I show up to inspect the boiler? It's not like she'll learn about her murder tonight, right?"

Zachary arched a bushy brow. "Elisabeth is letting you into the basement tomorrow?"

"Sorry, I meant to tell you earlier, but I got... preoccupied." Her mother's death had rattled her more than it should have, more than it had any right to do. "Are you free tomorrow morning to come with me?"

"Pending an emergency, I'm off all day, but why wait?" The sofa squeaked when he stood up. "Your grandmother deserves to hear the truth from you. If *Nurse* Darius learns about your mother's death, I don't trust him not to tell her in the worst possible way. Besides, the blood tests I ordered revealed a urinary tract infection, so I need to give her antibiotics. That's my excuse to tag along."

"Nana has a UTI?" *The infection could explain Nana's obsession with toilet paper.* "Is it the sexually transmitted type?"

Zachary extended one hand toward her. "No, but in the last twenty years, there's been a significant increase of STDs among seniors. If your grandmother is entertaining men at night, you may want to talk to her about safe sex."

"Me? You're the health professional, *Doctor* Zachary. It falls under your job description, not mine." Willow offered her hand, accepting his invitation.

His fingers wrapped around hers, awakening the dormant butterflies in her stomach. "Before we leave, I want to look at your hand."

Of course you do. Zachary possessed excellent bedside manners and a warm soothing voice, which should have reminded her he came here as a doctor—and not as someone or something else.

Chapter 6

Worried by her grandmother's lack of reaction to Brigitte's death, Willow knelt beside her rocking chair.

"Nana, did you hear me?" She patted her grandmother's frail hand. "Brigitte is gone, Nana. You won't see her or talk to her anymore. She's dead."

"He didn't want the baby." Unshed tears glistened in Nana's eyes. "The man in white killed her."

"Who's the man in white, Nana?" *A doctor, a priest, a ghost... a rich man in a white tuxedo?* "Did Brigitte tell you he killed someone? When was the last time you talked to her?"

Her grandmother stopped rocking and closed her eyes. "Leave me alone."

Willow exchanged a disheartened look with Zachary.

"Just get your grandmother to swallow this." Zachary handed Willow a pill. "Then you may want to tuck her in for the night. You can try talking to her again tomorrow."

Getting Nana to swallow the pill proved as challenging as finding a path through her failing mind.

* * *

The service elevator rattled going down into the basement of the nursing home, and its interior light flickered.

Zachary pictured Rose lying unconscious on the cold, rugged floor beside her walker. Her peculiar obsession about secret surgeries in the basement seemed to have compelled the octogenarian to seek answers on her own. As much as Zachary would like to provide Willow with answers, the reasons behind her grandmother's strange behavior might remain incomprehensible.

"Thank you for prescribing antibiotics that Nana only needs to take twice a day." Clad in washed-out blue coveralls, Willow held on to her toolbox with one hand and the railing with the other. "I'll come before and after work. That way I won't have to rely on Darius."

The same thought had occurred to Zachary. "So you know, I will explain her new regimen of medications to Darius and Elisabeth in detail and in person." These new prescriptions gave him an excuse to meet the nurse.

The elevator clunk coming to an abrupt stop, throwing him against the panel.

"Are you all right?" Her back against the wall, Willow had staggered without losing her footing. "I hate this elevator. I swear it's becoming more temperamental as the months go by."

No wonder Rose tumbled. "Willow, do you think it's possible your grandmother ventured in the basement and fell on the floor on her way up?"

The door screeched opened. Darkness and rattling pipes welcomed them to the basement.

"Pooping hell, I bet that's the noise Elisabeth is hearing." Exhaling loudly, Willow stepped out of the elevator and turned a small flashlight on, aiming the beam at the dirty concrete floor. "To answer your question, Nana pushes a walker. If she'd reached the basement, we'd see traces of it on the floor."

Zachary added his footprints to the many stamped in the dust and grim, but there were no signs of dotted or continuous lines. Her grandmother never exited the elevator.

The door closed behind him, grazing his back. *Someone needs to service that elevator before it traps someone in the basement.* "Tell me there's another exit."

"Sure..." A hint of amusement simmered in Willow's voice. "A narrow wooden staircase with rotten steps."

An uneasy feeling crept up his spine. He followed the beam of her flashlight traveling up a scratched wall to a switch with a missing plate.

"When looking for a switch, don't pat your way along the walls or you risk zapping yourself." She flipped the switch with her bandaged hand. "Do you need a flashlight or do you have one?"

Fluorescent tubes sizzled, flooding the corridor with white light. A suspended ceiling with yellowed tiles, all in dire shape, hung less than a foot from his hair.

"I have my phone." Along the corridor, half a dozen closed doors broke the symmetry of the walls. "Any idea where I should start?"

"Wherever you like. If you need me, the mechanical room is on the left at the end of the corridor. I may be in there for a while." A grimace contorted her face. "A long while."

* * *

Before he began his search of the basement, Zachary slipped on a pair of disposable gloves and tested the knob of the first door on his right. The metal was sticky, as if hundreds of greasy hands had touched it in the past. Dust had adhered to it, and it felt like it had never been wiped clean.

Glad he took precautions, Zachary pulled his phone from his pocket, turned the flashlight on, then pushed the door open.

A strong pungent stench assaulted his nose, testing his pharyngeal reflexes.

The room was jammed with warped boxes, scrap metal, a rusty bicycle, and an old mattress. He found the light switch behind the door and flipped it. Darkness didn't lift. He angled his phone toward the ceiling. No lightbulb was screwed in the socket.

Relying on his phone, he flashed his light across the room. Nothing specific caught his attention so he lowered the beam onto the floor. Two sets of distinct footprints had recently disturbed the dirt. His own size eleven boots and tiny little dots.

Appalled, Zachary tracked the pawprints to the edge of the mattress where a trail of mouse droppings led to a gaping hole in the discolored fabric. *These squalid conditions are unacceptable in a nursing home, or anywhere else for that matter. This is a serious health issue that Elisabeth needs to address in the immediate future.*

He checked the room on the opposite side of the corridor, encountering the same stench. A lone lightbulb illuminated the small room cluttered with filthy junk.

Someone needs to empty the rooms, take everything to the dump, and fumigate the basement. Dampness seeped through his coat, chilling him to the bones. Aside from the unwelcome rodents, no one had ventured in this room in a long time.

Something smashed onto the floor, startling him. The sound originated from further down the corridor. "Willow?" he yelled. "Is everything all right?"

"If everything was all right, I wouldn't be here in the middle of the night." Her frustration traveled down the corridor. "I need at least another fifteen minutes. Be careful, would you?"

"You too, Willow." Zachary opened a third door, subjecting his nose to another assault.

Among all the unrecognizable junk in the room, he spotted an old twin mattress. The rodents hadn't chewed their way into that one but the rusty spot on its edge suggested a bed bug infestation.

Invisible critters crawled on his skin. All the rooms contained a mattress. Zachary shuddered at the thought that these rooms once welcomed real people. *I doubt those poor souls felt fortunate to live in damp, windowless rooms in the basement.*

He flipped the light switch with his wrist and lost his grip on his phone. It hit the floor with a thud. Careful not to touch or lean on anything, he squatted down. The light from his phone shone through the missing slats of a wicker basket onto a metallic object. Its shape looked familiar. Still, it took his brain a few seconds to put a name on it.

A stirrup?

He lifted the basket by its handles. Its bottom fell out and the stirrup landed beside his phone. Stunned, Zachary picked them both up. The old cast-iron stirrup was heavier than its modern counterpart.

Invigorated by his discovery, he pushed the mattress aside, ready to comb through the junk behind it for remnants of a surgical bed. The mattress struck a box, collapsing its side and emptying its contents. Magazines spilled over the floor.

"Having fun making a mess?"

Startled by the sound of her voice, Zachary spun around. Willow stood in the doorway, holding her toolbox. A dark blotch smeared her left cheek.

"I haven't searched all the rooms yet, but I found something interesting." He dodged the magazines and approached her holding the object in plain sight. "Care to take a guess?"

Her eyes widened. "Is that a stirrup?"

"An old one." The object in his hand proved some sort of medical procedures had taken place in the nursing home a long time ago. "Your grandmother's delusion about secret surgeries and crying babies may hold some truth after all."

Something clunked.

"The elevator." A look of panic flitted across Willow's face. "If something fishy is going on, we can't be caught snooping."

The noise grew louder.

Zachary had smudged his footprints in the other rooms, but he didn't have time to blur them in this room. If anyone entered it, they would immediately realize someone had rummaged through it. "Too late. We need an excuse to be in this room."

"I..." She snatched the stirrup from his hand and shoved it in the large side pocket of her coveralls. "Do you trust me?"

"Maybe..." *Why do I have the feeling I will regret this?* "What do you have in mind?"

She left her toolbox in the corridor then closed the door, trapping them inside with the light on. Becoming more confused by the second, he blinked when she laced her arms around his neck.

"We could pretend we're..." Her eyes sparkled like gold, mesmerizing him. "We're taking a romantic break. It works in movies."

Heeding to her crazy idea, he wrapped an arm around her waist and pulled her into a tender embrace.

* * *

In the warmth of his arms, Willow breathed in his scent, a woodland scent that teased her senses. His lips gently pressed on hers and his hands stroked her back, unleashing waves of sweet and delicious

114

sensations. Lost in the kiss, she clutched his shirt losing her grip on reality.

A door banged against a wall.

Jolted, Willow recoiled, abruptly ending the breathtaking kiss. Had Zachary not held her, she would have fallen backward and landed on the floor.

"What's going on here?" Her fists on her hips, Elisabeth stared at them with an outraged expression. "Were you making out?"

Zachary dropped his hands and took a step back. "We're not... it's not... not what you think... not exactly." The man who'd swept Willow off her feet with a pretend kiss didn't meet her gaze nor Elisabeth's, but he looked adorable all flustered. "We were waiting for... for the elevator when one thing led to another and... and we ended up here."

A deep frown creased Elisabeth's forehead. "This isn't a hotel." She peeked into the room. "Look at the mess you made. Who's going to clean this up? And by the way, why are you here in the middle of the night?"

Ready to end the charade, which worked like a charm, Willow cleared her throat. "Sorry for the lapse of judgement, Elisabeth, but I came to tell Nana that my mother died. I wasn't sure how she'd react so I asked the doctor to accompany me. Right now I'm tired and upset. I didn't need to check the boiler. I did it as a favor because you complained about a weird noise, so the least you could say is *thank you.*"

The director lowered her hands down her sides, and for a brief moment, she looked contrite. "In light of these tragic circumstances, I'm willing to overlook this little incident. Will you bill me for your visit?"

No condolences? No inquiries about Nana's state of mind? Elisabeth's lack of compassion and empathy never ceased to amaze Willow. "Not for tonight. This was a complementary inspection, but I need to come back to replace a damaged coupling." Willow could have sworn she kept a spare spring-loaded coupling in her toolbox. "I'll check if I have a spare one in my garage. If not, I'll order one tomorrow morning, and hopefully it'll arrive by Monday."

"Very well." With a sharp motion of her hand, Elisabeth beckoned them to leave. "Good night."

"Since we're here, Director Brown, I would like to have a few words with you regarding Rose's health and the unsanitary conditions in the basement." In the blink of an eye, Zachary had regained his professional composure. "It shouldn't take more than half an hour."

The long sigh that Elisabeth exhaled betrayed her exasperation. She opened her mouth to speak, but after what appeared to be a long moment of mental deliberation, she acquiesced with a nod.

Willow followed them to the elevator, the stirrup weighing heavily in her pocket. *Nana may have been right about the surgeries in the basement. Maybe not in this decade, but at one point in the distant past.*

The door of the elevator opened.

Willow took a step back. "I think I left my screwdriver by the boiler." *Zachary hasn't checked all the rooms yet. I might as well keep snooping around while he talks with Elisabeth.* "Go ahead without me. I'll meet you in the lobby."

* * *

Zachary couldn't decipher Elisabeth's expression any more than he could explain her presence in the nursing home in the wee hours of the morning.

Her spartan office was located on the main floor. It contained a desk, a few chairs, a vertical file cabinet, and a freestanding coat rack. No picture frames or personal items.

After waiting in vain for an invitation to sit, Zachary took it upon himself to park his tired self in an armchair while he shared Rose's condition.

Her back to the file cabinet, Elisabeth glared at him. "I don't disagree with Rose's new drug regimen, but I don't appreciate being accused of negligence, Doctor."

He'd stated the facts regarding Rose without assigning blame, but it was obvious that Elisabeth felt targeted. "I'm not making accusations, but I'm concerned for Rose's health, for the health of every resident. Untreated infections of any kinds can lead to serious problems. I realize your nurse may be overworked and unable to monitor every resident in a timely manner, so I'd like your permission to examine the residents."

Silence fell on the office.

The digital clock pinned to the opposite wall had stopped keeping the time at 6:27. He wondered how long it had been since the batteries died, and if anyone noticed it was only right twice every day.

"Nurse Wiedrich takes his job very seriously, but you're right, there's just so many hours in the day." Elisabeth's conciliatory tone gave Zachary hope that she would agree to his request. "You're welcome to examine the residents but beware, they may not be as forthcoming as you think. As far as Rose is concerned, she never mentioned any discomfort to Nurse Wiedrich, or else he would have promptly addressed the issue before it turned into a nasty infection. No one, not even you, *Doctor*, can treat a problem if you don't know it exists."

Rose had complained in front of Willow and him, so Zachary found it hard to believe Darius hadn't overheard or suspected something was amiss. "I will apprise your nurse of the new regimen when I come back tomorrow. Wiedrich works on Saturday, doesn't he?"

A muscle twitched underneath Elisabeth's left eye. "Morning only. I will tell him you wish to speak with him. Will that be all?"

"No." The feeling he'd overstayed his welcome ruffled Zachary's hair as it flew over his head. "Regarding the conditions in the—"

"I know the basement is in disarray, but the residents don't live there, do they? They're not even allowed down there." The director crossed her arms and exhaled a noisy sigh. "I'll let you in on a little secret, Doctor. I don't have the money or the staff to clean the basement. My priority is on the two floors where the residents live, but you get me a grant or free labor, and I'll let you supervise the cleaning and the restoration. I have a waiting list longer than my arm, I could use these extra rooms and a new elevator. Now, if you can't help, stay out of my hair. I shouldn't have to remind you that my residents have nowhere else to go, unless you intend to accommodate the twenty-four of them in the hospital?"

The rhetorical question spoke of the lack of options for the residents. A roof, any roof, over their heads was better than none. "I understand the difficulties you're facing and I'm not trying to shut you down."

"Glad to hear." She pointed at the closed door. "The exit is that way, Doctor."

By no uncertain terms, he'd been dismissed. He could always attempt to question her about the four recent deaths, but he didn't want to risk annoying her any further. In the morning he would call Henry, the helpful clerk at the funeral home, and the only person who sounded willing to give truthful answers regarding the residents of the nursing home.

"Willow gave me a ride here." Zachary had offered to take his SUV, but since she came here to check the boiler, she'd insisted on driving her work van, which contained all her tools. "I'll see myself out, but I'll be back tomorrow morning."

Elisabeth yanked the door open. "Let me walk you to the lobby."

* * *

Willow didn't need to venture in any of the rooms. Opening the doors, inhaling the stench, and seeing the mess was enough to determine they more or less contained the same thing and probably served the same unknown purpose. A long time ago.

One last room to check. For the sake of thoroughness.

She turned the knob and pushed. Her shoulder hit the door. A locked door. The only locked door in the basement.

Determined to unearth the secrets that room was hiding, she pulled a hotel key card from her toolbox. The cards often came handy to scrape surfaces, but using one to unlock a door was a first.

She leaned against the door to widen the gap between it and its frame, slid the card in, and pushed. The latch bolt instantly retracted, and the door sprung opened. Caught off balance, Willow tumbled into the room and bumped into the leg of a table. Something shattered on the floor. The noise rang in her ears as she yelped in pain.

The light was on. Down on all fours, she looked around, reluctant to move. Shards of glass, some clear and some tainted blue, littered the floor. She winced lifting her injured hand. A clear shard was imbedded in her palm and blood reddened the bandage around it.

Great. Another injury. She debated pulling it out. *There are no major arteries running through my hands, right?* Where was the doctor when she needed him? *Elisabeth can't see me dripping blood, or else she'll ask questions.*

Short of a better option, Willow pulled the shard out. The bloodstain on the bandage didn't spread any further. Relieved her hand wasn't actively bleeding, she donned an extra glove to hide her new injury, then looked around.

A knot formed in her throat.

Burners and glass beakers of different sizes and shapes rested on a long rectangular table. Black hoses ran between the beakers, some empty and some with colorful liquids inside, and a ventilation pipe exited through the ceiling. The paraphernalia appeared to be in working order. Unlike whoever performed surgeries in the basement, the person conducting chemistry experiments hadn't retired yet.

Whoever runs that lab can't know I stumbled onto his illegal activities. Unfortunately for Willow, the broken beaker and the droplets of blood she'd donated on the floor were dead giveaways. *I'm never breaking into a room again.*

Hoping no one would notice a beaker went missing, she collected all the broken glass, dumped it in her toolbox, then wiped the floor with a rag, erasing any physical evidence linking her to this room.

This wasn't the sort of incident she could afford to report to the wrong person or tackle on her own unless she wanted to rejoin her late husband.

Rattled by the implications spinning out of control in her brain, Willow exited the room and hurried toward the elevator.

* * *

Zachary didn't appreciate being escorted out any more than he bought Willow's lame excuse for staying behind in the basement. Her toolbox was as organized as his surgical tray. He'd seen it open in his kitchen. Willow would have noticed a screwdriver was missing before she closed it.

The director paused at the entrance of the lobby. "Your ride is waiting, Doctor."

Looking displeased and eager to leave, Willow stood by the front doors, holding her toolbox with both hands. "Are you ready, Doctor?"

"Yes, he is." Elisabeth glared at both of them. "I take it you found your screwdriver?"

Willow answered with a curt nod. "Good night, Elisabeth."

Zachary muttered a disembodied farewell under his breath then quietly followed Willow into the cold night.

Once she drove away, he broke the heavy silence. "Are you angry at me for meeting Elisabeth afterward and having you wait for me, or for... for kissing you?"

"I could kiss you again for talking with her that long." An odd mixture of giddiness and elated relief sizzled in Willow's voice. "I'd just come back from the basement when you showed up. I didn't want Elisabeth to think I'd snooped around and found her secret room, so I tried to appear anything but suspicious of her."

Bewildered by Willow's rapid mood changes, Zachary searched her expression. Illuminated by the dashboard, she glowed with excitement. Growing more baffled by the second, he reran the weird conversation in his mind, trying to make sense of it.

Four words caught up with him. *Found her secret room.* Past tense. "What secret room?"

"The locked room at the end of the corridor, next to the boiler room." She glanced in his direction. There was no mistaking the triumphant smile on her pretty face, or the realization she wasn't mad at him. "Someone is running chemistry experiments in the basement, Zachary."

"You discovered some sort of drug lab?" Staggered by the revelation and possible ramifications, he sank into the passenger seat. "Did you take a picture?"

"No... it didn't even cross my mind. I was in a rush to pick up the pieces of the beaker I broke." She rapped her hand on the steering wheel, but the thick red and white mitten she wore muffled the beat. "I wiped my blood from the floor, but it's still going to show up during a forensic analysis, won't it?"

"*Your* blood? You injured yourself again?" Though he was happy to provide his services, he would rather spend time with her for other reasons. "Sorry, didn't mean to be overprotective. Your blood can be explained, so let's not worry about it yet. Could you please describe in detail what you saw in that secret room?"

* * *

In the safety of her home late at night, Willow sat at the kitchen table and peeled off her glove listening to Zachary's one-sided conversation with Constable Laforge.

The doctor recounted almost word-for-word what she'd told him in her van while also providing context to her discovery. "Did I see the lab with my own eyes? No, but I trust Willow. She has the glass fragments of a beaker in her toolbox. Her blood is on them, but you may still be able to lift fingerprints from the biggest fragments."

Heartened by Zachary's confidence in her, Willow returned her focus to her hand. The shard of glass had left a hole in the gauze that grew smaller with each layer she unwrapped, and so did the bloodstain, until the bandage no longer showed any hole or blood. "It can't be... It wasn't my blood."

"Hold on, Constable. I'm putting you on speaker." Zachary placed a hand on Willow's shoulder, capturing her full attention. "Willow, what do you mean by *it wasn't your blood*?"

"I heard a beaker shatter when I knocked the table, but the broken glass on the floor came from two beakers, one clear and one tainted blue, except I only heard one shatter..." A question Zachary had yelled resurfaced, sending shivers down Willow's spine. "Remember when you shouted asking if I was fine? I'd just heard something shatter on the floor. I thought it was you who..." The realization that they'd both attributed the noise to each other sank a brick in her stomach. "We were not alone in the basement, Zachary. I only broke one beaker when I stumbled into that table. Someone else had dropped the other one and shed blood. I fell on the bloody fragments of his broken beaker, not mine."

"Listen, you two." The constable's soft but commanding voice anchored Willow to reality. "My sergeant is listening to our conversation. He's indicating he'll send a team to check out the basement in the next hour or so. Stay home. Don't go back. An officer will stop by afterward to collect the bloody bandage and the glass fragments."

Chapter 7

Surprised by the chime of the doorbell, Zachary put his full coffee mug back on the counter and ventured into the vestibule to answer. He expected a call from Willow or Constable Laforge, not a morning visitor.

A chilly wind bit his face the moment he opened the door. "Willow?"

"I was under your third neighbor's trailer so I thought I might as well knock." Outfitted with a beige coat sporting yellow stripes, a yellow toque, and thick working gloves, she rocked back and forth in heavy boots. "I'm sorry if I'm intruding. I—"

"No, please come in. You look like a snowman... snowwoman." Delighted by her impromptu visit, he invited her in. "I just made coffee. Would you like a cup to thaw you out?"

"After spending what was left of the night worrying about what I'll do with Nana if the authorities shut down the nursing home, coffee would be great." The weariness on Willow's face resembled the one that was plastered on his before he shaved it off. "I'll drink it in the vestibule. I'm too tired to take my clothes off and too dirty to step into your trailer."

"Chester's trailer, not mine." Mice already infested the place. It couldn't get any dirtier. "You deserve to sit and rest. Just come in. I don't care about dirt, just mouse droppings."

She still took off her boots before following him in the kitchen. "Your furry houseguest has returned?"

"Yes..." Chester still hadn't responded to any of Zachary's emails. Reeling from his landlord's shady behavior, he placed a steaming mug of coffee on the table beside his notes on the four deaths at the nursing home. "How much would you charge me to seal the mice's entry point?"

"For you, nothing. For Chester, a fortune."

While Zachary wouldn't dream of not paying her, he pondered the option of asking her for a hefty written quote, which he would submit to Chester, or better yet, subtract from his next month's rent payment. *That would get his attention.*

Amused by her answer, Zachary ran the idea by her.

She hiccupped a chuckle as she unzipped her coat. "I can give you a quote, but it'll be a fair quote. As much as I'd like to add an annoyance penalty, it conflicts with my professional code of conduct. That being said, I will add a surcharge of twenty-six dollars, which is the amount he still owes me. I think that's reasonable." She took a sip then added milk to her coffee. "May I ask why you rented *this* trailer?"

Convenience. Laziness. And blind trust. "It was furnished and available right away. I didn't see myself driving into town without knowing where I would sleep."

In retrospect, he should have driven in homeless. The people in town had welcomed him with open arms and fed him. One of them would have invited him to stay on their couch until Zachary found decent accommodations. He didn't regret misplacing his sense of adventure as much as he did his faith in people.

His back to the refrigerator, he gulped a mouthful of coffee, but it didn't wash down the bitter taste lingering in his mind. "Renting the trailer was a mistake."

"At least you didn't buy it. If you ever decide to move, I can vet a few places for you." Her gaze traveled to the loose sheets of paper on the table. "Patient HY, GO, PT, and AM?" She frowned at him. "I realize doctors are supposed to maintain an emotional distance from their patients, but aren't letters a bit too impersonal?"

"I chatted with Henry, the clerk at the funeral home, about the other three residents of the nursing home who passed away recently. These are their initials." Zachary would only use random letters or numbers to identify patients if he needed to protect their identities. "Helen Yablonsky, Georgia O'Connell, Peter Tanguay, and Alphonse Morrison."

"So according to your clerk, Peter drowned in his bath after he slipped in the tub and bumped his head?" Willow picked up the sheet of paper titled *PT* and squinted. "He was... dunk?"

"Drunk." No autopsy had been performed, so Zachary couldn't rule out the patient had also been dunked.

"Wait a sec..." With her index finger, Willow tapped on the sheet where he'd scribbled *drunk*. "I don't know how or where Nana gets her information, but she told me one of the men who died drank poison on his boat and fell in the water. What if the boat represents a bathtub full on water? What if Peter drowned after tasting a potion from the basement? Could you exhume his body and request an autopsy?"

"I wish but all the patients were conveniently cremated." Unless Zachary managed to obtain someone's confession or testimony, *Accidental Drowning* would remain the official cause of death. "Did your grandmother say anything about the two women who died?"

"According to Nana, one woman was strangled by the ghost of her husband and the other was hit by a snowmobile while walking down the corridor." Willow shook her head recounting both scenarios then picked up the sheet labelled GO. "Georgia fell down the stairs and broke her neck after a resident in a motorized wheelchair lost control of his vehicle and bumped into her? Really?" Willow's brows furrowed in disbelief. "I'll make an educated guess here and say Georgia was the woman that Nana believes was hit by the snowmobile. Why does it say *frostbite* followed by a question mark?"

The clerk at the funeral home recalled the woman's son had objected to his dead mother wearing white gloves at her funeral, but Elisabeth had insisted, going as far as slipping the woman's wedding band back on over the fabric. The son had surrendered, but the weird incident had unsettled Henry. Thinking the gloves might serve to conceal obvious signs of abuse like broken fingers or cigarette burns, Henry had taken advantage of Elisabeth's absence to sneak into the mortuary room and peek at the dead woman's hands. He was shocked to see the fingertips on Georgia's right hand were dark purple, but unsure who he could trust, he'd remained silent.

"The fingertips of her right hand were dark purple." Zachary wished Henry had also sneaked a photo to corroborate his suspicion. "Georgia may have suffered from frostbite, which would imply she spent too much time in the cold without adequate protection. The snowmobile could represent the outdoors."

The myriad of contortions to which Willow subjected her facial muscles would have gained her entrance to a Mime Academy. To make matters worse, Zachary shared every emotion she displayed.

"I'm almost afraid to read how Helen allegedly died." Willow rummaged through the sheets of paper then recovered the one labelled HY. "Helen died of asphyxiation after being discovered with her head trapped between her mattress and box spring? Somehow that doesn't sound any more plausible than being strangled by a ghost. Was something stashed under the mattress to explain why she stuck her head there in the first place?"

Zachary had asked that same question, but the clerk couldn't provide him with any more details. "No clue, nor do I know who made the grim discovery. Needless to say, none of these alleged accidents were investigated."

"This is starting to resemble Brett's death." Willow tossed the sheet on top of the others then grabbed her coffee cup with both hands. "A boatload of suspicion but no proof."

Nurse Camille had suggested that Willow might have played a role in her husband's death, but Zachary refused to listen to rumors, not after they almost destroyed his reputation. He didn't doubt his nurse meant well any more than he doubted Willow's story. The hunting scene rang true.

Regardless of how these four nursing home residents died, there wasn't anything Zachary could do, but he would be damned if he let anything unnatural happen to any of the current residents. "Did an officer pick up the evidence before you were called out this morning?"

"Yes, Constable Laforge stopped by while I ate breakfast. She collected everything and swabbed my cheek to compare my DNA against the blood on the bandage, not that she didn't believe me, but she wanted to be thorough. In her place I would have done the same. I... I also told her about your half-cooked theory about my extra finger."

"Well done," he quipped, pleased with her decision. "What did she say?"

"She asked more questions about my father, none of which I could answer. She couldn't give me an update on the search of the basement, but when I drove by the nursing home on my way here, I glimpsed someone searching the dumpster." Leaning back in her chair, Willow sipped on her coffee. "I found a coupling in my van while I was fixing your neighbor's trailer. Not sure how it ended up in the wrong drawer, but I'll be able to fix the boiler as soon as we're allowed in."

Her phone rang.

Willow frowned at the screen before answering. "Hello?" Her expression softened. "Good morning Constable Laforge.

I'm alone with Dr. Auckerman. Would you mind if I put you on speaker so I don't have to repeat everything?"

"Sure." Laforge's chortles rose in the kitchen. "Unfortunately, I don't have lots of good news. The search was a bust. Director Brown was on the premises when we arrived to inspect the basement. She said the doctor had warned her that the contents of the rooms constituted health hazards, so she'd already started disposing of the junk and cleaning the rooms. She begged my sergeant not to shut down the nursing home for the sake of the residents."

"Elisabeth begging?" The director's bogus distress only confirmed what Zachary suspected. "Elisabeth Brown twisted my words to her advantage, using them as an alibi of sort, but she has to be involved in whatever is going on."

"I'm not disagreeing, Doctor, but Brown is doing a great job at washing away any evidence. Two of the basement rooms were emptied and thoroughly cleaned prior to our arrival. We smelled the disinfectant the moment the door of the elevator slid open. We think the lab was dismantled shortly after you discovered it. What happened to the drug paraphernalia is anyone's guess, but it wasn't thrown in the dumpster." A hint of frustration pierced Laforge's words. "With any luck, the glass fragments or the blood will give us a lead, but until more evidence surfaces, there's not much we can do. On the bright side, we believe you're all safer than you were yesterday."

"Safer?" The foregone conclusion flew over Zachary's head without brushing his hair. "We blew the whistle. How's that supposed to make us safer? Or stop Elisabeth, or the mad chemist, from retaliating against Willow's grandmother?"

"Director Brown knows the RCMP is now involved. If she threatens anyone, she'll be under even more scrutiny, which is something she'll want to avoid at all costs. Her only option is to put her money where her mouth is, clean all the rooms in the basement, and pretend the secret lab was a figment of someone's imagination." The constable's arguments appeared sensible, even though Elisabeth might not be. "I'll touch base with you later. Now if you'll excuse me, my bed is calling me."

"Thank you, Constable." Willow hung up and slumped in her chair. "I tipped Elisabeth of my discovery when I picked up the evidence. I screwed up."

"No, you didn't. Whoever broke the other beaker may have seen me snooping around. Remember how upset Elisabeth was to find us in the basement? Maybe she feared we'd already stumbled on the lab, and decided to dismantle it at that moment. The evidence you collected proves it existed before it vanished." Zachary shuddered thinking Willow had stayed behind and could easily have encountered the chemist.

"When I talked to Elisabeth last night, I told her I would come back this morning to examine patients. I'll enlist Nurse Darius's help, so I can also assess his competence."

"That should be fun…" She returned her mug to the counter. "Since you're heading that way, I might as well finish the repairs on the boiler this morning. When are you planning to leave?"

"Whenever you're ready."

* * *

Zachary didn't like the idea of Willow working alone in the basement, but he wouldn't dare voice these objections. The woman wreaking havoc with his heart and mind was inhabited by remarkable strength and determination. She would undoubtedly chew his head off if his overprotectiveness curtailed her independence.

Notwithstanding the knot twisting his stomach, Zachary observed the nurse shadowing him during his visit at the nursing home.

Darius's stylish dark hair, accentuated by the loose strand hanging over his left eyebrow, gave him a devilish but professional appearance. The crispy indigo scrubs he wore didn't sport a single stain and the blood collection tray he carried didn't display any scuff marks, or items out of place. With his pristine kit and impeccable scrubs, Darius resembled a rookie on his first assignment.

The woman whom Zachary examined suffered from hearing loss. A hearing aid she refused to wear unless she watched television was set aside on a small coffee table near her rocking chair. Though she ignored most of his inquiries about her health, she agreed to let him draw a blood sample.

Darius presented him with the tray. "Here you go, Doc."

Stunned by Darius's bold presumption, and eager to test his nursing skills, Zachary cocked his head and stared. "You're not my caddy, Nurse Wiedrich. Collecting blood specimens falls within your job description, so get to it."

* * *

Relieved to have escaped the basement of the nursing home unscathed, Willow made herself a cup of tea before sitting at the kitchen table in front of her computer.

She clicked on the nursing home account to add the cost of the coupling and the time it took her to fix the boiler. Knocks on her door interrupted her mental debate about adding the cost of the N95 mask she wore to filter the overpowering odor of disinfectant.

"I'm coming." She didn't expect anyone, but when she opened the door, she couldn't resist a smile. "Zachary? I see you survived your morning with Darius?"

"Contrary to the rumors I heard, the arrogant prick is actually skilled, but I'm leery of the kind of care he provides when no one is looking over his shoulder... I shouldn't have said that out loud." Looking anything but apologetic, Zachary handed her a box of pizza. "I wasn't sure if you'd eaten yet, so I brought lunch. Half all-dressed, half Hawaiian."

The smell wafted through the vestibule, triggering her hunger. "This will be delicious. Thank you."

"You're welcome." He took off his winter gear then followed her into the kitchen. "Were you working? Am I disturbing you?"

"I was just sending an invoice to Elisabeth for this morning services. It can wait after lunch." She set the pizza on the table and invited him to sit. "Did you come here to eat so your mouse wouldn't steal a slice? Or did you discover something interesting during your rounds?"

Amusement twinkled in his eyes. "I could come up with an excuse for being here, but I was hoping I didn't need one."

If she didn't know any better, Willow would again swear that he was flirting with her.

"Why aren't you married, Zachary?" She regretted inquiring the moment the question

138

escaped her lips. The phony kiss they'd shared didn't give her the right to probe in his private life. "I'm sorry. I'm not usually that blunt. It's just... you're kind, honest, compassionate, and cute. Many women around here would kill for a man like you. Please, feel free to stop me before I make a complete fool of myself."

His laughter filled the kitchen, dispersing the awkward cloud hovering above her head.

"Just so you know, men like to be complimented from time to time too. And for the record, disarming honesty is one of the many qualities I admire in you, so to answer your question, I was engaged once. Louise cheated on me with a colleague hooked on opioid." Zachary grew more somber with each word he uttered. "After one of his patients died as a direct result of his addiction, I reported him. I'd gathered compelling and irrefutable evidence against him, but his lawyer accused me of vendetta over his affair with Louise. As a result of my testimony, my colleague's medical license was suspended. I was absolved of any unethical behavior, but it left my personal life in shambles and my professional life marred with hard feelings. Not everyone agreed with my decision to expose the truth, but I couldn't turn a blind eye. I didn't want the death of his next patient on my conscience."

Willow admired his commitment to his patients, but she also knew from experience that personal relationships were complicated, even after they ended. "Do you still love her?"

"No, there were many red flags in our relationship, but I was too busy working to notice them. The trial exposed all the lies and the ugly truth. The right woman is out here. Somewhere." Zachary met her gaze. "How about you? Would you be willing to give real love another chance? And have dinner with a boring and overworked guy?"

"Boring sounds appealing right now." *And overworked sounds strangely familiar.* "I wouldn't say no to dinner, or real love." As a teenager, she'd mistaken lust for love. The possibility of experiencing real love was both exciting and terrifying. "Any chance that boring guy could look beyond my past and my family's reputation?"

"Boring guy wouldn't change a single thing about you, Willow." His sultry voice caressed her ears. "Are you free for dinner tomorrow night?"

On Sundays, she only dealt with emergencies, and charging twice her regular rate ensured they were real emergencies. "Tell your boring guy to come around six tonight. I'll make him supper."

Chapter 8

On Sunday morning, Willow knocked on her grandmother's door.

"Nana? It's Willow." When no one answered, she unlocked the door and entered. "Nana, are you there? It's time to take your antibiotics."

The bed was unmade, the room was empty, and the bathroom door was closed.

Wary of her grandmother's whereabouts, Willow peeked into the bathroom first. The shower curtain was drawn. "Nana?"

Something thumped and squeaked behind her. Startled, Willow spun around.

Her grandmother tottered out of the closet holding on to her old walker. "The girl with six toes is in the bathroom. I can't go pee." A puddle formed between Nana's bare feet. "I want to go home."

"Nana..." Willow refrained from asking Nana when her diaper was last changed. Her grandmother was sick, physically and mentally, and she needed additional care, not a lecture on hygiene. "You need a bath.

I'll get the water running. Please don't move."

Having no desire to wipe and disinfect the entire floor, Willow hurried in the bathroom, push aside the shower curtain, and froze.

Swollen rolls of toilet paper were breaking down in the cloudy water filling the tub.

Willow sighed in dismay. *When did I sign up for this nonsense?*

* * *

After enjoying a quick breakfast during which he didn't see any of his furry houseguests, Zachary drove to the hospital. His head nurse wouldn't approve of his visit on a Sunday, but he could no longer ignore the strange fuss that Willow's mother made around her daughter's finger.

A security guard played solitaire on a table in the lobby. Zachary nodded at him then walked by the deserted nurses' station. According to the schedule affixed to the desk, Nurse Heather was on duty, but she was nowhere in sight.

Zachary locked himself in his office to avoid being disturbed while he accessed the provincial health database, starting with Willow's record since he needed her mother's full name.

"Your mother is Brigitte Ruth Mitchell and your father is unknown. Let's see what I can find about your mother..."

The database contained five women named Brigitte Ruth Mitchell, two named Ruth Brigitte Mitchell, and one named Brigitte Mitchell Ruth.

"Which Brigitte are you?" Zachary eliminated the women who died before last week and all the ones who weren't of childbearing age when Willow was born. In the end, two women remained.

The first Brigitte Ruth Mitchell lived in Mississauga, a city in the Greater Toronto Area. Eleven months ago, she was diagnosed with breast cancer. Since then she'd received chemotherapy and underwent a mastectomy. Her prognosis was good, but she didn't fit the description of Willow's mother.

The second Brigitte Ruth Mitchell lived in Ottawa. She was forty-three years old and hadn't been declared deceased yet, but it was possible her record hadn't been updated.

"Willow's grandmother is eighty-four years old. She would have been forty-one when that Brigitte was born. The Ottawa Brigitte would have been nineteen when Willow was born. The timeline belongs in the realm of possibility." However, Zachary didn't learn anything useful from that Brigitte's record.

Having hit a brick wall, he walked into the lounge where Nurse Heather ate a muffin.

"Doctor?" Crumbs peppered the front of her teal scrubs. "Weren't you supposed to take the weekend off? Angela will bite my head off if she learns I let you stay when the beds are empty."

Though Angela occupied the position of head nurse, when it came to seniority, Nurse Heather beat all the hospital employees by many years. If anyone knew about old hospital records, it would be her.

"I'm not here to see patients." *Not unless an emergency arises.* "I've started visiting the residents of the nursing home, but I hit a snag. Some of their records aren't available online." He hadn't updated the records of the patients he examined yesterday yet, and while his current interest lay in Brigitte Mitchell, Zachary anticipated encountering difficulties retracing some of these older residents' records. "Is there an archive room somewhere in the hospital?"

"Oh yes, there is. You don't really think the government would let us shred anything, do you?" The matron rolled her eyes then gestured for him to follow her into the wing where the lab was located. "It's in the basement, last room on the right."

Of course it's in the basement. Where else would old records be relegated to? After his misadventures at the nursing home,

Zachary almost dreaded venturing into another basement.

The doors of the elevator next to the lab parted. Following a short and smooth descent, he exited into a large corridor illuminated by bright fluorescent bulbs and paved with cream speckled tiles.

On each side of the corridor, pale yellow doors broke the monotony of the long white walls. They were all closed and unmarked.

The contrast with the basement of the nursing home couldn't have been more pronounced.

Marching down the corridor, Zachary peeked into the rooms. Some were empty, others contained boxes. "What is the purpose of these rooms?"

"Your guess is as good as mine, Doc, but it's a shame they aren't used. When he built the hospital, the contractor went over budget, so the government cut funding for whatever extra equipment was supposed to be acquired. Over the years, the basement turned into a huge storage area." She pushed the door adjacent to the emergency exit staircase. "Here we are."

Row upon row of storage racks bolted to the floor and fastened to the suspended ceiling occupied the room. The shelves were stacked with boxes in different shades of white, beige, or gray.

Zachary noticed some gaps here and there on the shelves and two empty racks, which appeared to divide the room in three unequal sections. "Is there a system?"

"All the records on the left of this rack have been converted into digital documents and downloaded into the database." The nurse patted the empty rack on the left then moved toward the other empty rack. "This middle section contains the records of the patients who've visited the hospital in the last ten years but whose records haven't been converted yet. And the right section contains anything older than ten years."

Willow is twenty-four years old... The answers he sought might be relegated to the right section. "Do these last records go back before the hospital was built?"

"You bet they do." Nurse Heather parked her plump body on the low desk pushed in the corner of the room. "For nearly fifty years, Dr. Holloway operated the only clinic in town. It had a rudimentary surgery room, a lab, a few beds, some basic equipment, and it never closed. A nurse was always on duty. Twenty-four hours a day, seven days a week. I was fresh out of nursing school when I started working there. That was a long time ago." Her gaze lost its focus traveling down memory lane. "Over the years, other doctors came to work at the clinic, and while they never stayed long, they also generated lots of paperwork. After the hospital was built, Dr. Holloway moved his practice in here. The records, documents, test results, notes, bills, receipts... everything from his old clinic was packed into these boxes. The medical records of the returning patients were pulled out and ended up in the other two sections, but nobody ever bothered sorting out the remaining contents of the boxes."

Energized by the knowledge nothing had been discarded, Zachary was eager to browse through the boxes. "This is perfect, Nurse Heather. I'm optimistic I'll eventually find the records I'm looking for."

The nurse sprang to her feet. "If you give me the names of some of the elderly residents, I can help you search."

Until he developed a better understanding of the situation and identified the players and their motives, Zachary preferred not to involve anyone else in his secret activities.

"I appreciate the offer, Nurse Heather..." He shoved his hands in his pockets while searching his brain for plausible excuse to refuse. Except for his car keys, his pockets were surprisingly empty. "I left my tablet and my phone in the car. What was I thinking coming in without their names?"

Nurse Heather burst out laughing. "If you ask me, Doc, you're working too hard."

"Maybe you're right, though I'm certain the same applies to you." He gestured for her to follow as he left the room. "I'll go get my tablet, but you should take advantage of the quiet day to relax in the lounge. Doctor's order," he quipped. "I promise to yell for help if I end up buried in here."

"We're lucky to have you, Doc." The nurse smiled, stepping into pace with him. "I speak on behalf of the entire staff when I say we will all do our very best to ensure you stay in Ojibson. So please, don't hesitate to ask for anything."

"That's very kind. Thank you." Zachary was touched, but he refused to take advantage of their desperation. "As you know, I spent a great deal of time at the nursing home yesterday. The building looks older than the residents. Has it always housed older folks?"

"No." The furtive glance she threw his way projected strong feelings. "It started as a residential school, an historical fact that the elders in the community haven't forgotten. As you probably noticed yesterday, indigenous residents are scarce, and I can't blame them. The government should have torn the building down instead of recycling it over and over again."

The lack of ethnic diversity among the nursing home residents had indeed struck Zachary as odd, but he would never have guessed it to be related to the original mandate of the decrepit building. "How was it recycled?"

"Sanitarium, residential school, maternity home for unwed mothers, convalescence center, treatment center for drug or alcohol addiction…" She jabbed the button of the elevator with her elbow. "They changed the name and the purpose of that building more times than I can remember, but it never eradicated the despair impregnating its walls."

The door parted. Deep in thought, Zachary stepped in behind his nurse. The old stirrup he found could date back to the time the building served as maternity home.

How did you know about the surgeries in the basement, Rose? Were you a witness, a patient, or a victim? Learning the history of the building didn't answer any of his questions, it only added another layer of mystery.

* * *

Willow understood scheduling, but denying breakfast to an old lady because she entered the dining room ten minutes too late was the crack that burst the pipe.

After fetching a breakfast sandwich, a muffin, an orange juice, and a coffee at A&W, and making sure her grandmother ate and drank something, Willow marched into Elisabeth's office. "We need to talk."

The director frowned lifting her head from the documents scattered on her desk. "Ever heard of knocking, Mitch?"

Ever heard of feeding your residents? Willow swallowed the reply before it increased the tension in the office. "I had to give Nana a bath because she peed in her

149

nightgown. By the time I walked her to the dining room, breakfast was over—by ten minutes. Your cook wouldn't even give her a slice of bread or a banana. Correct me if I'm wrong, but I was under the impression it was someone's job to ensure Nana ate, either by taking her to the dining room or bringing her a tray." Seething with indignation, Willow struggled to keep her voice steady. "No one came to check if she was awake, dressed, or breathing. Is that the quality of care she receives on a daily basis? Does she eat on the days I don't visit her?"

Her hands clasped together on her desk, Elisabeth held Willow's heated gaze. "I do not appreciate being accused of negligence, Mitch. My staff and I are working hard to make sure all the residents receive the care they deserve." Elisabeth's definition of *deserve*, which didn't match Willow's, should be revisited unless the director believed some residents were more deserving than others. "After I saw you come in, I told my staff not to intrude on you and your grandmother. I incorrectly assumed you would provide her with the assistance she needed." The assumption sounded like a lie, a flat-out lie. "The schedule and the menu for the week are clearly posted on the wall at the entrance of the dining room. I understand you encountered an unforeseen delay, but I would appreciate it if you didn't blame the cook. Some residents used to take advantage of him by showing up late all the time, so he was instructed to make no exceptions. That being said, I apologize for the misunderstanding and the inconvenience it caused you and Rose. It will not happen again."

Considering everything else that is going on here, do you really expect me to believe you? Even though the dispassionate and condescending lecture exacerbated her outrage, Willow knew better than to wage a losing battle, verbal or otherwise. "It cannot happen again, Elisabeth. If you're not equipped to deal with Nana, I'd like to know so I can make other arrangements."

"I'll personally reassess your grandmother's condition and ensure she receives more adequate supervision." The glint in the director's eyes unsettled Willow. "Will that be all?"

* * *

Propped against the dresser in Nana's room, Willow observed her grandmother.

Nana rocked in her chair, staring at the ceiling yellowed by years of smoking and neglect.

Her cognitive abilities had worsened at an accelerated pace in the last few months, but Willow wasn't sure if she should attribute the steep decline to the normal progression of the disease ravaging her mind or the dark events occurring within the walls of the nursing home. Regardless of the answer, Nana had reached a new milestone. She needed additional care.

What am I going to do with you, Nana? Willow couldn't afford around the clock home care any more than she could afford to stay home. *I have to work to pay the bills.* "I want you to be safe without taking away your freedom or dignity, Nana, but I can't bring you home. I wish there was a nicer facility—"

"I don't like it here." Amid the squeaking of the chair, her grandmother gazed at her with a faraway look in her eyes. "The child is mean."

I'm sorry, Nana, if you think I'm the mean child. "If I had more money, I would take you home, but—"

"You have money, Brigitte." Her grandmother stopped rocking. "In the secret account for the imperfect girl."

The insult thrust yet another invisible dagger in Willow's chest. Not trusting the words seeking escape from her mouth, she rode the familiar wave of pain, sorrow, and disappointment in silence. The nature of her relationship with her family would never change, but she refused to let it define the woman she became, which was the reason she took care of her grandmother. *For my own sake. To prove to myself that I'm more than the sum of my DNA.*

Once the dull ache faded away, the meaning of her grandmother's tirade struck Willow, shining a ray of hope on their situation.

She knew nothing about a secret bank account, but it made sense her mother had stashed her *earnings* somewhere. Years ago, an account had contained enough money to buy a house. Whether it was depleted or replenished remained to be determined, but as next of kin, Willow stood to inherit Brigitte's assets.

Even if Brigitte wrote a will in which she disowned her only child, Willow clung to the hope that provisions were made for her grandmother.

* * *

Disappointed that his morning search of the archive room didn't yield any results, Zachary left the hospital.

Willow was born in Ojibson. The records of her birth should not only exist but also be readily available. That he couldn't find any reference to Brigitte aroused his suspicions, boosting his resolve to keep combing through the records of the archive room.

He drove to the nursing home and bumped into Darius upon arriving. The nurse followed Zachary's every move throughout the afternoon, projecting an aura of overconfidence and intimidation. The nursing home residents appeared edgy, uncomfortable in Darius's presence, more so than yesterday.

Couldn't you have taken this afternoon off, Darius? Voicing the request would have undoubtedly roused the nurse's suspicion, so Zachary hid his mistrust and misgivings behind the caring expression he showed every patient. Still, he made a mental note of contacting the Ontario Nursing Association to inquire about Nurse Darius's status.

At the end of the day, Zachary was glad to bid farewell to his last patient and escape the suffocating atmosphere of the nursing home.

Once seated in his car, he messaged Willow.

On my way to the hospital to drop the samples I collected this afternoon. See you in twenty minutes.

He didn't encounter anyone in the lobby of the hospital. No one manned the nurses' station, the lounge was deserted, but moaning and groaning could be heard from the exam rooms. He dropped the samples to the lab then went on to investigate the commotion.

"Doc?" Nurse Camille caught up with him in the corridor. "I was about to call you.

We have a nine-year-old boy curled up in pain in Exam Room One. It looks like an appendicitis attack, his second in two months."

The boy's condition sank a brick in the pit of Zachary's empty stomach. From the sound of it, he might end up performing an emergency appendectomy at one point this evening. Regardless of the outcome of his examination, by the time he finished running the necessary tests and reached the right diagnosis, it would be too late for dessert.

This wasn't his first romantic evening to fall victim to his work, nor would it be the last. Still, he hadn't felt this disappointed in ages.

"I'll be there in a minute, Nurse Camille." He pulled out his phone from his pocket. Asking Willow to wait for him in case he might show up later on for a nightcap seemed unfair and unreasonable, and served no other purpose than ruining both their evenings. "I just need to cancel my dinner date with Willow."

Chapter 9

Zachary's long morning shower didn't wash away his fatigue. "I'm getting too old for all-nighters."

His phone rang while he got dressed. "Yes?"

"Morning, Doc. It's Camille. A toddler swallowed Lego pieces." A child screamed in the background, obscuring the nurse's voice. "She doesn't have any breathing issues, but her mother is hysterical for fear of losing her custody to her ex-husband."

"I'll be there in ten minutes." He grabbed a bagel and drove away.

The sun peeked over the horizon, casting a weak light over the fresh layer of snow blanketing the unplowed streets and the parking lot of the hospital. As usual, he parked on the last row and briskly walked inside, the cold air reenergizing him.

In the lobby, patients had already started lining up for their morning appointments. Zachary acknowledged their presence with a nod of the head before heading toward the nurses' station manned by Nurse Camille.

"Sorry for the call, Doc." With her unbuttoned coat on her back, Nurse Camille looked ready to go home. "Did you get some sleep?"

"Yes. Some." *Just not enough.* Zachary stowed his keychain and his gloves in the pockets of his winter coat before removing it. "How's the toddler?"

"Not as distressed as her mom. They're in Exam Room Two with Heather." Nurse Camille took his coat. "I'll hang it in your office."

* * *

The beeping of her phone interrupted Willow's breakfast. The name or phone number of the sender didn't appear on her screen, but the message enlivened her morning.

> *No hot water. Can you come fix my tank now please?*
> *Doc*

"Doc?" The signature tickled her. "What happened to Zachary, Doc?"

After replying she would show up in ten minutes, Willow forked the last morsel of omelet in her mouth and downed her cup of coffee. This was her first emergency call of the day, and she didn't any have jobs scheduled until this afternoon. His timing was perfect.

She missed not seeing him last night, but she understood emergencies. If she wanted their budding relationship to stand a chance, she had to accept the reality that she would always have to share him with his patients.

An unfamiliar silver car was parked in Zachary's driveway. It didn't resemble Chester's or anyone else she knew. Willow parked behind it. As she walked past it, she felt the heat emanating from the hood. The car's presence didn't confound her as much as the absence of Zachary's SUV.

She knocked on the door.

Seconds later it opened, revealing a woman wrapped in a large blue towel.

Shocked by the apparition, Willow eyed the number on the door then looked behind at the street sign. As she squinted to read the recognizable name, a white truck turned the corner. It slowed down driving by the house and a man sharing a striking resemblance with Chester stared her way, accentuating her confusion and embarrassment.

Once Willow managed to refocus her attention on the half-naked woman playing havoc with her emotions, her identity hit her. *Camille. The nurse working at the hospital and daughter of a former math teacher.*

"Sorry for the service call, Mitch. Zachary didn't realize I'd already taken my shower when he got up." Giggles shook her bare shoulders. "Next time I'll make sure to leave some hot water for him. He just left to deal with an emergency, but he wanted me to give you fifty dollars for your trouble." The pretty nurse presented Willow with some bills. "I would appreciate if you didn't tell anyone I was here. There's a woman infatuated with him and he's trying to shake her off gently by pretending he's spending his evenings at the hospital when in fact he's with me. He's so thoughtful."

Confusion made room for disillusionment then anger, the nauseating deceit sullying Willow's dignity. The doctor had taken her for a ride, and like a fool she'd believed every word he said.

Feeling like a cheap version of her mother, Willow refused the money and left.

* * *

What on earth did I do with my keys? Zachary needed the pair of running shoes he kept under the passenger seat in his SUV.

His first patient of the morning, an eight-year-old girl complaining of stomachache, had hurled two-day's worth of digested food onto him. Covered from shoulders to toes with vomit, Zachary had taken a shower in an empty patient room after the consultation, then donned a set of blue scrubs with matching shoe covers. He didn't mind the scrubs but hated the idea of walking barefoot in the shoe covers.

Brushing and rinsing his work shoes hadn't eliminated the offensive odor, so he wanted to chuck them in favor of his old running shoes, but his vehicle was locked.

I could have sworn I put my keychain in my coat pocket upon entering the hospital.

His two gloves were still tucked inside, one in each unzipped pocket, but his keys were missing. If they'd fallen on the floor, he liked to believe that someone would have heard a tinkling sound and picked them up.

After searching his office to no avail, he retraced every path leading to the nurses' station. Nothing.

Out of desperation, he recruited Angela's help. While she combed the area around the nurses' station, Zachary inched toward the entrance, his gaze scanning the floor.

A shadow entered his peripheral version. He snapped his head up and came to an abrupt halt before colliding with Nurse Camille and becoming the unfortunate recipient of a spilled coffee.

"Hey, Doc, are you looking for something?" An air of satisfaction enveloped the nurse. "It's been a tough night, so I brought you breakfast and coffee."

Touched by her thoughtfulness, he accepted the offering. "Thank you, but I'm also looking for my keys. I have a feeling they fell from my coat pocket. You didn't happen to stop anywhere with my coat, did you?"

"I—" A muscle twitched at the corner of her left eye. "I couldn't find my phone, so while I looked for it in the lounge, I put your coat on the couch. Maybe your keys fell between the cushions. I'll go look for them."

She rushed into the lounge under Angela's quizzical look.

The head nurse pointed at the breakfast in Zachary's hands. "She likes you, Doctor Zachary."

On a professional level, Zachary liked all his current nurses, but on a romantic level, he wasn't interested in Nurse Camille. Besides, he would never pursue two women at the same time. "I'm seeing someone, and Nurse Camille is aware of my relationship with that woman."

"Then I suggest caution." Angela glanced back and forth between him and the doorway of the lounge. "Camille is an only child and her parents doted on her. What Camille wants, Camille usually gets. It doesn't seem to matter what—or who—stands in her way."

It's too bad Nurse Camille didn't get the job at the nursing home. Zachary could have avoided crossing paths with her on a regular basis and he wouldn't have to worry about

161

the care provided to the residents. "Well, she'll be disappointed."

Seconds later, Nurse Camille emerged dangling a familiar set of keys. "I found these behind a cushion. Are they yours?"

* * *

Willow didn't know what shocked her the most when she visited her grandmother at the nursing home around suppertime. To find Nana seated in the dining room in a nice dress with her hair styled and the fresh scent of citrus lingering in her wake or to receive a text from the doctor. A text that started with *I miss not seeing you—*

Startled by a tap on her shoulder, Willow lost her grip on her phone and fumbled to catch it before it fell in her grandmother's plate, a plate filled to the rim.

"Sorry, Mitch, I didn't mean to scare you." Her hands clasped together, Elisabeth eyed the elderly ladies around the table like a hawk. "As you can see, we adjusted the level of care provided to your grandmother. There will be a slight increase in her monthly fees, but since I can always count on you to come right away when we have plumbing or heating issues, I worked out a reduced rate. You can call it a loyalty discount. Will that be acceptable?"

For the second time today, Willow felt like she was offered hush money, but this time she couldn't decline the offer, at least not until she found better accommodations for her grandmother. "I must say I'm pleased with the changes, Elisabeth. Thank you."

Ignored by her grandmother who chatted with her dining companions about a cat with patchy fur, Willow excused herself and drove home.

Once she entered the house and closed the curtains, she finished reading the doctor's text.

> *I miss not seeing you yesterday. I wish I could cash in on that raincheck tonight, but I have a patient who suffered a massive heart attack. I need to stay here. Enjoy your evening. Zachary.*

Aghast, Willow read the message twice. For a man who wanted to get rid of her, he not only took the scenic route but also got lost in the wilderness. His twisted game irked her. She couldn't believe how badly she'd misread him. *Well, Doctor, I will make it easy for you to dump me.* During her marriage with Brett she'd suffered enough humiliation to last her a lifetime. She replied to his message.

Don't worry about me, I'm busy all week, and the weekend doesn't look any more promising.

She didn't have anything planned for the weekend yet, but she would find something to do that didn't include the doctor.

Sorry about your patient.
Willow

If the patient existed, she didn't bear any ill wishes toward him or her, but Willow was disappointed and hurt that their new doctor used the suffering of others to play with her. A tiny voice inside her head insisted that something was wrong, that something didn't add up, but the image of the naked nurse blurring her mind silenced it.

Sending the message reminded her of the call she'd received this morning. The lawyer taking care of Brigitte's affairs wanted to meet with her at the earliest opportunity. Taken back by the request, Willow had told his secretary that she would check her schedule and call back.

Once the autopsy was over and Brigitte's body was released, arrangements would need to be made regarding her funeral. Her apartment would need to be emptied. And a mountain of paperwork would undoubtedly need to be filled. Unless Brigitte relegated these tasks to someone else in her will, as next of kin, they fell on Willow's shoulders.

I need to talk to that lawyer.

* * *

Mystified by Willow's lukewarm response to his text last night, Zachary meant to talk to her in person before heading to work, but a fierce collision between two snowmobiles required his immediate presence at the hospital.

A woman wearing the colors of the volunteer fire brigade directed snowmobiles pulling sleighs through the ambulance loop. "Morning, Doc. We have five injured, all ejected from their seats, even the two kids riding in the sled behind mom and dad's snowmobile. The one in worst shape is the teen driver. He wasn't wearing a helmet when we found him tangled in the branches of a spruce. One of my guys and one of your nurses already brought him inside."

"He's in Exam Room Two, Doc." Nurse Heather picked up a sobbing child from one of the sleighs. "His name is Joshua. He has a reputation of drinking too much and driving too fast."

"Great..." Not impressed by the irresponsible young man, Zachary marched into Exam Room Two where his patient was connected to a monitor. "How is he, Angela?"

"Unconscious. Blood pressure is elevated, heart rate is low, breathing is shallow, he reeks of alcohol, and something is embedded in his skin above his right ear. A piece of bark or branch..." Angela cut a strand of blond hair matted with blood. "The bleeding has stopped, but I'm afraid it'll start again if I remove it, so I'll leave you the honor."

Treating an injury that could have been avoided by a helmet wasn't an honor, but it was Zachary's job.

The family of four was discharged two days later, but it took an extra twenty-four hours before the teenager was released into the custody of a RCMP. During these three days and nights, Zachary didn't see or hear from Willow, but he learned from the rumor mill that she would be traveling to Ottawa on Friday to lay her mother to rest.

The news shed a different light on her lukewarm response. With everything that had happened in the last few weeks—her grandmother's failing health, the machinations at the nursing home, her mother's murder, and the ramifications of all these events—describing herself as busy had been an understatement. Willow projected such a strong and brave front that Zachary had failed to notice how physically swamped and emotionally drained she must have felt.

166

For a doctor who rarely misses a sign, Zachary, you completely blew up that diagnosis. Too busy with his own work, he'd asked for another raincheck when she needed a hug, a shoulder to cry on, a sounding board, or all of the above. *I'm sorry, Willow. I get it if you're angry with me. And if you're not, maybe you should be.*

He would give her another day or two before texting her again. In the meantime, he would spend his evenings in the archive room searching for any information regarding her mother. Willow deserved to know the truth about her origins.

With these resolutions in mind, Zachary finished updating his last patient's file. The big analog clock on the wall indicated 7:03 p.m.

He grabbed his coat, opened the door, and paused. Standing still with her fist in the air, his nurse gaped at him.

"Nurse Camille?"

"I... I was about to knock." She lowered her arm down the side of her parka. "My shift is over. I was wondering if you'd like to share a bite to eat with me... or talk about Joshua or Mr. Cosset, your heart attack patient in ICU."

The teenager would face the consequences of drinking and driving. That Joshua didn't kill himself or any members of the young family when he plowed into them at sunrise was nothing short of a miracle. As far as Mr. Cosset was concerned, he'd lost a brave but desperate battle in the middle of the night.

There's nothing to talk about. There was nothing Zachary could have done differently, nothing that could have changed either outcome. "Thanks for the invitation, Nurse Camille, but I don't socialize with my staff outside the hospital. Please, don't neglect your boyfriend or your family on my behalf," he added to shift the awkwardness on him. "I'm not worth the trouble."

"I..." Nurse Camille didn't cast her gaze away, but she appeared to ponder her answer, giving him hope that she'd read between the lines. "To be honest, I was looking for an excuse not to have supper with my parents tonight. I guess I'll have to come up with a different reason. Enjoy your evening, Doc."

* * *

On his lunch break on Friday, Zachary sent Willow a text wishing her a safe trip to Ottawa. The northern segment of the route could be treacherous under any conditions, but more so during the winter.

His phone rang, forcing him to bottle up his worries. "Dr. Auckerman speaking."

"Good afternoon, Doctor. I'm Sandra Hamel at the Ontario Nursing Association." She didn't sound like the same woman he'd talked to a few days back. "You inquired about a nurse by the name of Darius Wiedrich working at a nursing home in Ojibson?"

"Yes, I did, Sandra." Pleasantly surprised by the callback, Zachary grabbed a pen and a notepad. "I'm not doubting Wiedrich's qualifications as much as I'm questioning his peculiar behavior. Can you tell me if he's registered with you or if any complaints have been filed against him?"

"We have a Darius Wiedrich registered with us..." The woman mumbled something about overdue fees. "His record is unblemished. If he displayed any questionable behavior during the twelve years he's worked at Kingston General Hospital, no one reported him."

His perfect record doesn't mean Darius wasn't guilty of any wrongdoing. It only means he hasn't been caught yet. Still, the timeline struck Zachary as odd. With his baby face, Darius didn't look a day older than twenty-five. Unless he finished his nursing degree before he grew hair on his chin, Darius couldn't have worked anywhere for twelve years before moving to Ojibson. "I wasn't aware of his previous employment. May I ask what you mean by overdue fees?"

"I probably shouldn't tell you this, but Nurse Wiedrich hasn't renewed his membership and paid his yearly fees yet." She lowered her voice. "He's always stayed in good standing, and we never had to charge

169

him any late fees in the past. It's probably why his file hasn't been updated to reflect his current position at your nursing home."

A nurse with more than twelve years of experience shouldn't forget to pay his professional dues—unless he has money issues. "Does that mean Wiedrich isn't allowed to practice? Or was he granted an extension?"

"If he doesn't pay by next week, his membership will indeed be suspended. He won't be allowed to practice until he renews, and if he doesn't renew by the third week of March, his membership will expire. I'm sorry I couldn't enlighten you more on his behavior."

"I'm grateful for the information you provided. Thank you." Zachary hung up then dialed the Kingston General Hospital.

Chapter 10

On Saturday afternoon, Zachary showed up at the nursing home to examine more elderly residents, but as Elisabeth had once predicted, many remained guarded and unforthcoming despite Darius's absence. It felt as if someone had cast a dark shadow over their spirits.

Disheartened, Zachary recalled his earlier conversation with Dr. Crocker, a geriatrician at Kingston General Hospital. *Darius quit his job last June. He was qualified but unprofessional. His departure wasn't a big loss for the geriatric department.*

Qualified but unprofessional was a step above unqualified and unprofessional. Still, the residents of the nursing home deserved better.

* * *

Exhausted on every level, Willow enjoyed a long bath in her hotel room.

Her phone, which she'd left on top of the closed toilet lid, rang. A part of her wanted to hear from him, but the number didn't belong to him. "Yes?"

"It's Constable Laforge. I'm sorry for calling you on a Saturday night, Ms. Mitchell, but I'm in town. Any chance we could talk in person?" The constable wouldn't request an in-person meeting unless it was important. "It shouldn't be too long."

"I wouldn't mind, but I'm not in Ojibson right now." If the constable had called ahead, Willow could have saved her the trip. "I won't be back from Ottawa until tomorrow afternoon."

"You're in Ottawa?" The news appeared to have taken the constable by surprise. "May I ask the purpose of your visit?"

"I had a meeting with my mother's lawyer yesterday afternoon. He's her legal executor, and as it turned out, I am her sole beneficiary." Brigitte didn't disown her only child, but she also didn't leave a lot in her will. Only three bank accounts. The furniture in the condo hadn't belonged to Brigitte any more than the condo itself or her sports car. "We met again today to finalize her last wishes. Why?"

"If the detective in charge of your mother's murder would have known you were in Ottawa, he would have arranged to meet with you instead of delegating that task to me. I'm on duty at the detachment tomorrow. Any chance you could stop on your way back to Ojibson?"

Laforge's insistence to meet in person unsettled Willow. "How about telling me right now what's going on? That way I won't stay awake all night worrying about what transpired."

"Well... It's about the DNA found under your mother's fingernails." The constable's reluctance to speak impregned every word she spoke. "It... it shares some of your paternal DNA."

Flabbergasted by the revelations, Willow sank in the tub. The water rose to her neck. "Are you saying my birth father killed my mother?"

"If it were your father, he would share all of your paternal DNA, not just some." The distinction between some and all implied their suspect was a paternal relative. "The DNA was female. An aunt or cousin of yours fought with your mother. She may not have meant to kill her, it could have been an accident, but until we talk to her, she's our best suspect. Growing up, do you recall hearing anything about your father's family?"

"No..." *Just hurtful rumors about my mother.* "How... how did you match her DNA to mine?"

"The swab I took the day I collected the bandage. Once your DNA is entered in the system, it becomes available for all searches. Listen, Willow, I'm—"

"Please stop." By discovering the lab, Willow had given the police a suspect, but she needed time to process the murderous additions to her family tree. "I'm fine." *I will be fine.* "Were you able to identify the blood on the bandage?"

"The DNA analysis indicates your chemist is closely related to Fergus Lynch, a felon currently serving a fifteen-year sentence for murder at Millhaven Penitentiary. According to his record, Lynch doesn't have any siblings or children, but his father visits him once a week. Problem is, Dad is ninety-one years old and bound to a wheelchair. He wasn't the one in the lab that no longer exists." Laforge expelled a heavy sigh. "So, to answer your question, we have no idea who that blood belongs to, but there's more. Yours and your mother's DNA are tied to a cold case. Forty-four years ago, a man in his early twenties died after the car in which he was a passenger collided with a moose in Newfoundland. The driver was identified by his family, but they had no idea who was the young man in the passenger seat. His photo was circulated throughout Newfoundland then the Maritimes. A few leads were investigated, but they all came to a dead end."

Collisions with moose happened every winter, but that particular accident at one end of the country didn't trigger any recollection. "I'm almost afraid to ask what the connection is."

"We would need your grandmother's DNA to confirm it, but everything indicates he could be your mother's father."

"My what?" Brigitte died at forty-three. The man in question could technically have fathered her before he died, but— "That man cannot be my grandfather. My grandmother was over forty years old when she had my mother. The idea she had an affair, or even a one-night stand with a man young enough to be her son is ludicrous."

Something resembling a chuckle coursed through the line. "Sorry, I didn't mean to laugh, but in my line of work, a younger man getting an older woman pregnant is a credible scenario. If I send you his photo, would you show it to your grandmother? Please? That young man deserves to have his real name engraved on his tombstone."

* * *

Zachary spent his Sunday in the archive room of the hospital.

An inner closet he hadn't noticed on his previous visits was packed with boxes stacked on top of each other with no shelves in between. The heavy weight of the many rows had damaged or crushed the boxes resting on the floor.

He searched each box then scribbled a few keywords related to its contents on its side. Though it wasn't included in his job description, he hoped one day to have time to sort them out.

A corner of the box he was moving split open, spilling ultrasound images. The last names followed by the first initials of the patients were listed at the top. As he browsed through them looking for Mitchell, he stumbled on a unique name. A name spelled in capital letters without any initials attached to it. A name he'd previously noticed on some blood results. AKNA.

His curiosity unleashed, Zachary entered the name in the web browser of his phone hoping it might reveal an acronym of some sort.

"Let's see..."

The first hit was for AknaCase, a company making iPhone cases, but the iPhone didn't exist back when that ultrasound was taken.

The second hit was on Wikipedia. *Akna, goddess of fertility and childbirth in Inuit mythology.*

The slim connection between ultrasound, fertility, and childbirth prompted Zachary to pull the image out of the pile so he could look at it in its entirety.

Upon seeing the name penned down in black marker at the bottom, his heart skipped a beat. *Brigitte.*

Mystified by the misleading discrepancy between the goddess's name at the top and the handwritten first name at the bottom, Zachary scrutinized the image. According to the annotations, the patient was eight weeks pregnant. On the left side of the image, an embryo the size of a raspberry was visible at first sight.

Zachary compared the embryo's due date to Willow's birth date. Hers occurred six days earlier than the embryo's due date.

"The timeline adds up. You're little Willow."

Baffled by the pseudonym assigned to her mother, Zachary dug out all the documents, reports, results, anything about AKNA, and stashed them into a spare box without reading them.

Once he gathered all he could find, he returned home.

* * *

Zachary chased the mouse from the kitchen table then spread the documents on top, sorting them by chronological order.

The first record contained the results of a blood test done fifteen months before Willow was born. In the months that followed, a thorough medical exam was performed along with extensive tests and blood analysis.

If Brigitte had visited Dr. Holloway, which Zachary surmised she'd done as a child or teenager considering she grew up in Ojibson, those records had disappeared. *What happened, Holloway? Did you erase any traces of Brigitte's existence before she became AKNA?*

The hospital staff and the patients alike praised the late doctor for his dedication and selflessness. For Holloway to be involved in any deceitful scheme seemed unimaginable, and yet his name or signature appeared on every piece of paper.

Zachary read the annotation at the end of the report.

Candidate shares striking resemblance with wife. Excellent chances of healthy pregnancy.

Unsettled by the terms used, Zachary envisioned a few different scenarios, but to some degree or another, they all sounded like a surrogacy transaction. As he progressed along the timeline, a clearer picture emerged.

An anonymous sperm donor from Ottawa, referred to as *Husband* in the notes, sent a shipment of fresh semen to be used to artificially inseminate AKNA upon arrival.

Many annotations were made about the procedure.

> *Courier delayed twenty-four hours. Temperature-controlled storage box damaged during transport. Sperm unviable/unusable. Notified husband and wife. Recommended skipping a month and waiting for next shipment. Brigitte insisted—*

"Brigitte?" The slip confirmed AKNA's real identity.

> *—on going through the motions. Afraid not to be paid. Went ahead and injected sterile water instead of unusable sperm to avoid any infection.*

"Nice of you to care about Brigitte's health, Holloway, but which one of you was afraid not to be paid?" Almost wishing he hadn't discovered the truth, Zachary kept reading.

Three weeks later, the doctor had administered four pregnancy tests, two days apart of each other. They all came back positive.

"It's impossible." Zachary stared in shock at the results of the four pregnancy tests. Water alone couldn't impregnate a woman. "Brigitte was already pregnant. That's why she insisted to go through the motions."

Holloway's next annotation mirrored Zachary's suspicion.

Already   pregnant?
Father?

* * *

Under normal circumstances, Zachary wouldn't stop uninvited at anyone's home on a Sunday evening, but a particular signature on a legal document demanded he made an exception.

He knocked on her front door. The woman he sought answered with the phone glued to her ear. Her surprise to see him morphed into obvious delight.

"Sorry, sis, my doctor just paged me. I need to go to the hospital. Bye." Nurse Heather shoved the phone into the pocket of a worn-out green housecoat. "Thanks for rescuing me, Doc. My sister is riddled with problems, all of her own making, and I'm the only sibling who still listens to her. Sometimes I wonder why. Come in."

After removing his boots, Zachary followed her into the living room. "I need your help."

"For you to visit me at home, it must be important." She invited him to sit on a love seat the same shade as her housecoat. "What can I do for you?"

From the inside pocket of his coat, Zachary pulled a photocopy of a page from AKNA's medical records. "I've been looking for Brigitte Mitchell's medical record. It's been eluding me so far, but I found this Notice of Live Birth in a file named AKNA. I'll admit giving a surrogate the name of a fertility goddess was a nice touch. I believe the witness signature at the bottom is yours?"

The moment Nurse Heather laid eyes on the document, her demeanor changed, becoming more guarded by the second. "That was a long time ago."

"This is Willow Mitchell's notice of live birth, isn't it?" The baby's name wasn't listed on the form, only the gender of the newborn and her date of birth, which coincided with Willow's birthday.

"Yes, it is." His nurse's expression remained cautious. "Is there a reason you're stirring the past? You do realize that once you know something, you can't ever unknow it?"

The truth destroyed illusions, but it also exposed the lies. "Dr. Holloway and Brigitte Mitchell are dead, but whatever secrets they protected didn't die with them. They're buried in the basement of the hospital. Don't you think Willow deserves to hear the truth from us before an ill-intentioned individual hurt her with it?"

"What Willow would have deserved is a mother, and a grandmother, who wanted her." Crushed by an invisible weight, Nurse Heather sank into the recliner next to the fireplace. "Rose is as much to blame as Brigitte, but Willow still takes care of her. Despite her rotten family tree, that girl has a heart of gold."

"Then start by telling me about her grandmother." Rose's medical record was full of holes and didn't mention the birth of a daughter, so Zachary might as well start with the trunk, then climb up the branches.

"Rose was a teacher. Very strict, very sanctimonious. She never married and didn't retire until she was in her mid-sixties, but she loved strays. Humans and animals. She loved shaping them, molding them... I was in her class and..." His nurse clasped and unclasped her hands. "Let's just say, the kids got lots of bruises whether they fell from the monkey bars or not. We were afraid of her and felt sorry for the girls at the Maternity Home who also had to endure her lessons. Believe me, those poor girls didn't need any more hardship."

Spending time at the maternity home with the young mothers-to-be would explain the crying babies and basement surgeries. Rose could be revisiting her past. "Where does Brigitte fit in her life? Did Rose adopt her from the Maternity Home?"

182

"I'm not sure Brigitte fit in Rose's life any more than Willow did." A strange shadow crossed Nurse Heather's eyes. "By the time Brigitte was born, the Maternity Home had already become a Convalescence Home, but they were still many single women who stayed there to rest, shed weight, and get rid of their responsibilities. So yes, there were probably newborns available for adoption, but if you're an intransigent, single woman in her early forties, who dislikes unruly children, would you adopt a crying newborn?"

If Zachary had harbored Rose's feelings toward children, which he didn't, he would have avoided to adopt or raise any. "Are you saying she birthed Brigitte?"

"Back then, Rose was a heavy woman. It would have been easy for her to conceal a pregnancy, not that I understand why she would keep her baby instead of giving her up for adoption." Nurse Heather shrugged. "In the end, the how or why Brigitte came into Rose's life isn't important, but it defined who Brigitte became. That girl was smart, headstrong, beautiful, and cunning." Nurse Heather's gaze traveled to the large painting above the mantle. In it, fierce ocean waves battered a rocky shore in all their beautiful hues of blues and greens. "Brigitte stopped at nothing to get what she wanted. I don't know how she ended up being a surrogate at eighteen, but she was recruited and paid by the couple who wanted her to carry their child, not by Dr. Holloway. It's no wonder something went wrong."

"Like giving birth to a child with six fingers?" Prior to the Assisted Human Reproduction Act of 2004, there was no laws surrounding surrogacy. Agreements relied on good faith, and breaches were almost impossible to enforce. "It's a trait that Willow could only have inherited from her birth father."

"If not for that extra finger, the truth might never have come out." Nurse Heather briefly closed her eyes. "I was assisting Dr. Holloway with the delivery. You should have seen the shock on his face when he saw the baby was born with six digits. He didn't say anything, but I could tell he realized right away that the baby wasn't the result of artificial insemination. From there, everything unraveled. Dr. Holloway was devastated. He once told me he'd only agreed to the procedure in exchange for new equipment. He felt genuinely sorry for ruining the baby's life, not that it was his fault that Brigitte strayed."

The couple had enlisted Holloway's help to have a child. Granted, Brigitte's baby ended up not being biologically related to the husband, but it wouldn't have been related to the wife one way or another. The couple could still have adopted Willow.

Human behaviors never ceased to baffle Zachary, but then Dr. Holloway's motive struck him. "What do you mean by new equipment?"

"Dr. Holloway was a decent man who dedicated his life to his patients." Her voice softened. "I know it sounds cheesy, but he's the reason many underprivileged kids in town attended college. I was the youngest of nine children and my father died when I was sixteen. If Dr. Holloway hadn't subsidized my education, I wouldn't have become a nurse. I owe him my career, and my loyalty, but I wouldn't lie to cover his activities, or anyone else's. The clinic desperately needed new ultrasound and x-ray machines. Those are expensive pieces of equipment. The doctor couldn't get the funding he needed, so he sought donations where he could."

"Did he receive the donation he expected in exchange for his surrogacy services? Or did the couple renege on the payment?" Zachary's opinion of Holloway slightly improved. Some doctors wouldn't have resisted the temptation to fatten their bank accounts instead of giving back to the community. *No wonder the old town doctor is held in such high esteem.*

"The couple donated the machines, but the doctor never spoke of them again. I never knew their names, and I don't know anyone with extra digits. Whoever got Brigitte pregnant did her and her baby a great disservice. Dr. Holloway tried to convince Brigitte to surgically remove Willow's sixth finger and give her up for adoption, but she refused. Instead, she dumped her baby in Rose's arms then took off god-knows-where with god-knows-who. Rose was sixty years old and still teaching. She was no more interested in raising her granddaughter than I was in running a marathon." Nurse Heather expelled a shaky breath. "Brigitte also asked for her medical record, all of it. Since you found files related to AKNA, I'm guessing Dr. Holloway only gave her the files with her real name on it. Maybe you're right. Maybe he wanted the truth to see the light of day."

Something in her medical record had either made Brigitte nervous, and she wanted to remove any evidence of it, or had made someone else nervous, and she intended to exploit it. "Is it possible her medical record contained controversial information, like the name of a former lover?"

"Your guess is as good as mine, Doctor, but every time Brigitte rolled into town in a new sports car, reeking of money, Rose welcomed her with open arms." Bitterness clouded Heather's eyes. "It made me sick to see them suddenly develop a relationship when neither bothered to bond with little Willow. No wonder the girl eloped at sixteen. She just wanted someone to love her."

No kids deserved that kind of upbringing, but the more Zachary learned about Willow's past, the more infatuated he became.

* * *

During her drive back from Ottawa, Willow wrapped and rewrapped her mind around the notion that one of her female relatives, a relative that Willow never knew existed, was somehow involved in her mother's death.

She missed not talking to Zachary, not bouncing scenarios on him, but she lacked the courage to clear the misunderstanding between them. A part of her wished she hadn't suggested they kiss in the basement. At the time it had seemed like a good subterfuge, and she could have sworn he enjoyed it as much as she did.

I can't believe I misread him so completely. No wonder her love life sucked.

By the time she entered Ojibson, the sun played hide and seek among the treetops. The clock on the dashboard read 7:14 p.m.

She should have arrived hours ago, but a traffic accident in which she wasn't involved, had closed the road for almost three hours.

Exhausted after spending the previous night turning and tossing, Willow was ready to crawl into bed and sleep for days.

She drove by the hospital. A few vehicles were scattered in the parking lot, but the doctor's blue-green SUV wasn't among them. At the next intersection, she veered left on a whim. She had no clue what she intended to prove by driving in front of his trailer, but it didn't stop her from glancing at his driveway. It was empty.

Dejected, Willow headed home.

If he were making a house call, she'd rather not know what kind. Or to whom.

* * *

Galvanized by his enlightening discussion with Nurse Heather, Zachary returned to the hospital.

Only a few boxes had contained old receipts for expenses related to equipment. At the time, he didn't pay much attention to the receipts, but he applauded his decision of writing the contents on the side of each box.

In the soothing silence of the archive room, he checked the boxes he'd labeled *Receipts - Equipment.* In the third box, he found the pertinent receipts.

A new x-ray machine ordered ten months before Willow's birth was delivered two months later, and a new ultrasound machine ordered the week of her birth was delivered three weeks later.

The names of the recipient, Dr. Holloway, and the provider, Medi Solution from Montreal, were listed at the top of both receipts. A red stamp apposed over the price read *Prepaid In Full*, but the name of the generous couple was nowhere to be found.

If Zachary could identify the couple, they might provide valuable insight in Brigitte's life at that time of her recruitment, pointing him toward a possible boyfriend or lover. It was a long shot, but one worth investigating.

He dialed the phone number listed for Medi Solution.

"Medi Solution. Mon nom est Wendy." A human voice answered in French. "My name is Wendy. Comment puis-je vous aider? How can I help you?"

"Oui... Good evening." His French was too limited to attempt a proper greeting, but to hear the company was still in business and provided bilingual customer service on a Sunday night pleasantly surprised him. "I'm Dr. Zachary Auckerman. Twenty-four or twenty-five years ago, you sold ultrasound and x-ray machines to a generous couple who gifted them to our remote medical clinic in Ojibson, northern Ontario. We'd... we'd like to honor that couple for their lifesaving gift with a plaque, but no one seems to remember their names." Lying didn't come naturally for Zachary, so he was glad the woman at the other end of the line couldn't see his face. "Any chance you could help me identity them?"

"The purchase records should still be in our database." The woman's confidence heartened him. "Do you have the name of the clinic? The unit serial number? The—"

189

Zachary hated to interrupt, but he wanted to cut to the chase. "I have two receipts with all this information in front of me."

"Sweet." Her exclamation drew a smile on his face. "What are the receipt numbers?"

"The two receipts start with B as in Bravo, M as in Mike, Four, Seven, Three, Nine, One, One." He enunciated slowly. "The first one ends with C as in Charlie, Eight, Eight, and the second with D as in Delta, One, Nine."

The woman repeated both numbers then put him on hold. The silent seconds stretched into minutes.

"Thanks for waiting, Doctor. The ultrasound machine was bought by Mr. John Brown and the x-ray machine by Mrs. J. Brown. There's no address or contact number listed. Don't ask me if they were related. Your guess would be as good as mine."

If asked, Zachary would guess the couple hid behind one of the most common surnames in English-speaking countries. One the other hand, he knew one Brown who lived in Ojibson.

Chapter 11

Taking advantage of her quiet Monday morning, Willow paid her grandmother a visit and found her in the bathtub, her head peeking over white foamy bubbles. The faraway look in her eyes, the glow on her face, and the peaceful smile gracing her lips spoke of blissful contentment.

Concerned over the amount of water underneath the bubbles, and the inherent risk of drowning, Willow knelt by the tub and dipped a hand into the water opposite her grandmother's head, grazing her toes. The water, hot enough to clean a greasy bowl, stopped less than two inches from the edge of the tub. "Nana, who poured you a hot bath and how did you step in?"

"I did. That's my job."

Startled by his voice, Willow spun around dragging her hand in the water and splashed the nurse who'd sneaked up on her.

Darius glanced down at his wet scrubs, then at the bundle of sheets he carried in his arms.

"I... I'm sorry." Despite her apology, Willow expected him to rebuke her, but to her surprise his expression didn't sour.

"I suppose I deserve it for scaring you, which I can assure you was not my intention. I thought you'd seen me by the closet when you came in." He tossed the bed sheets on the floor by the toilet. "Rosie, would you like to soak for another ten minutes while I redo your bed, or are you ready to come out and go for breakfast?"

"I like water. I want to go on a boat ride and have a picnic." Nana blew on the bubbles. "Clouds are coming. Is it going to rain?"

"It's snowing outside, Nana. Not raining." Flabbergasted by the surreal situation, Willow bolted to her feet to face the man whom she wouldn't trust to give a dead dog a bath let alone a living human being. "What's going on here, Darius? What are you doing in Nana's bathroom?"

"Like I already told you, I'm doing my job." He turned his back to her and walked out.

Afraid to take her eyes off her grandmother, Willow stood in the doorway. From there, she kept both of them in her line of vision.

The nurse whipped a crispy clean white sheet on Nana's bed. "Had you come to visit your grandmother over the weekend, I would have informed you that her incontinence has worsened. You did request

192

additional care and services for her, didn't you?"

"You're the one bathing her, dressing her, and combing her hair?" In her wildest nightmares, Willow would never have imagined that Darius would be the one helping Nana with her personal hygiene. "Isn't it the job of an attendant?"

"In case you haven't noticed, the attendants are overworked. When Elisabeth asked me to ascertain your grandmother received the best possible care, I decided to personally take care of her." He finished the bed then walked back into the bathroom. "Rosie and I are now best buddies, aren't we Rosie?"

"He's such a cute boy, Brigitte." Nana smiled. "He gives me flowers and candies."

"Candies? What kind of candies?" Less than impressed by the arrangement, Willow pointed her index finger at the nurse. "Are you drugging my grandmother?"

"The only drugs in her system are the ones prescribed by *your* doctor." Some eight inches taller than her, Darius swept her hand away. "The candies she refers to are the tablets she uses to clean her denture. You're lucky I caught her before she put one in her mouth. This is also why the box is in my pocket and no longer in the drawer. I'll drop a tablet in her denture bowl after I put her to bed every night."

Something happened here during her trip to Ottawa, something that changed her grandmother's and Darius's behaviors, changes so drastic they sounded deafening alarms in Willow's ears. "I appreciate the extra care you're providing, Nurse Wiedrich." The words burned Willow's tongue, but she forced them out as smoothly as she could.

"Is that so? Does that mean you're done making false accusations? Can I trust you to keep an eye on your grandmother while I take the dirty sheets to the laundry room?" A predatory leer lifted the corners of his mouth, instilling distrust and fear. "I would rather she didn't drown on my shift."

"So would I, Nurse Wiedrich."

Once the money in Brigitte's accounts was transferred into hers, Willow would be able to move Nana into a better facility, or bring her home and hire a full-time attendant.

Willow waited for the nurse to leave before kneeling by the tub and showing her phone to her grandmother. "Nana, look at the screen. Do you know this man? He died in a car crash around the time you were pregnant with Brigitte."

"He's a cute boy." A dreamy expression floated over Nana's face. "I want more candies."

Disheartened by her grandmother's ambiguous answer, Willow put her phone away. "Time to get out of your bath before you're more shriveled than a raisin."

* * *

On his way to the hospital, Zachary made a detour by the funeral home. "Good morning, Henry the Helpful," he quipped entering the building.

The clerk didn't rise from his chair but he still greeted Zachary with a smile. "You just missed Mrs. Brown, Doc. She left for the nursing home five minutes ago."

Good timing. Zachary had counted on her absence. "I actually came to see you, Henry. As you can probably imagine, I hear lots of stories from my patients, but sometimes it's hard to tell if they're telling the truth or pulling my leg. You've been here what? Forty years? What can you tell me about Mr. Brown?"

"Forty-four years." The clerk sat back in his chair puffing his chest. "Mr. Joe Brown hired me when I was eighteen. After he suffered a stroke, Mr. John Brown took over. I'm guessing he's the one you're curious about?"

John. Same first name as the generous donor. "Yes. What can you tell me about his marriage to Elisabeth and his death?"

"He married late. He was in his forties, she was in her late twenties. They never had children. I don't know how Mrs. Brown felt about children, but he didn't want any. He'd embalmed one too many." The clerk cast his gaze down. "At times I wondered why Mr. Brown got married in the first place and to a much younger woman to boot. He was always here, working. Day and night. The funeral home was his life."

"Did John ever live in Ottawa, even for a short period of time?" The semen shipment wouldn't have come from Ottawa if the donor had lived in town.

"Mr. Brown leaving town?" Henry shrieked, visibly horrified by the suggestion. "He hated to travel, unlike his wife. Back then, Mrs. Brown drove to Ottawa once a month to visit her brother the judge. Her trips became less frequent after he moved to Toronto, but that was also around the time Mr. Brown died. She was busy with the funeral home."

Despite their names, the Browns didn't fit the profile of the couple seeking a surrogate. "How and when did John die?"

"An outsider started a brawl at the old Moose Pub and a fire erupted. That was close to twenty years ago. The pub was rebuilt and renamed the Antlers Pub. Between you and me, I never understood why Mr. Brown was at the Pub that night. He didn't drink or smoke." Henry pulled a bottle of clear liquor from a drawer. "Vodka. Would you like a glass?"

"No, thanks." Zachary's poison was beer, not vodka, and he only indulged on vacation. "How many people died in that fire?"

"Mr. brown was the only one who didn't

come out alive. Every man, woman, and child watched the pub burn down. People were shocked, angry. They blamed the outsider, chanting *Lynch Lynch Lynch*. The guy is lucky the Mounties arrested him before the crowd lynched him in the street." The clerk poured himself a glass. "You won't tell Mrs. Brown about the booze, right?"

"Of course not." Zachary was a doctor, not the vice squad. "Did the RCMP charge the outsider?"

"For what? Drinking too much? Yelling insults? Being stupid? I don't think anyone knew for sure who threw the first punch, but the guy was an outsider, the obvious scapegoat." Henry downed his glass. "My father used to say *it takes two to tango*. That night, the entire town danced."

* * *

Distrustful of Darius's intentions, Willow made a surprise visit to the nursing home after lunch.

The inside lock on her grandmother's door was gone. It could only be locked and unlocked from the outside. Like a prison cell.

Although Willow was shocked she wasn't consulted, she couldn't deny her grandmother couldn't be allowed to roam freely anymore.

Dressed in a yellow blouse and green skirt, Nana rocked in her chair. Alone. No straps tied her wrists or ankles to the wooden frame. Yet.

Willow knelt in front of her. "Brigitte is gone, Nana."

Brigitte's last wishes were for her body to be donated to a medical school where young doctors would play with her organs. The wording in the will had disgusted Willow. Nonetheless, she'd told the lawyer to comply with her mother's wishes.

"I donated her body to science." It saved Willow from arranging a funeral that no one would attend. "You won't see her again, Nana."

"The wrong baby was born." Her grandmother's voice sounded as chilly as the wind pounding on the living room window. "It's all her fault."

"Which baby, Nana?" Unsure how far in the past her grandmother had regressed, Willow patted her withered hand in a futile attempt to bring her back into the present. "Whose fault is it?"

"The girl with six toes." Nana's crooked fingers curled into fists. "He knew…"

While the incessant obsession with her extra digit tested Willow's patience and compassion, she couldn't help wondering about the *he*. "Who knew what, Nana?"

"The father…" The last time that Nana had used the word *father* in a sentence, it was to yell at Willow for asking about him. "He couldn't be the father…"

"Whose father, Nana? Is it mine?" It frustrated Willow to know the answers were locked in her grandmother's mind, but no one was in possession of the key. "Did he have a sister?"

"No one knows she has six toes." Her grandmother unclasped her fists. "The drug dealer messed up Agnes's room."

The sudden tangent threw Willow for a loop no more or less twisted than her grandmother's mind. *I hate riddles or puzzles with missing clues or pieces.* "Who's Agnes? Where does Agnes live?"

"I want to go home, Brigitte." Nana's head drooped on her shoulder, and she closed her eyes. "I'm tired."

Me too. For a moment, Willow envied her grandmother for living in a world where she didn't have to face the harsh reality of present time. "I'm looking into taking you home, Nana. Just hang in there, and please, don't eat any candies."

* * *

Zachary took the call that his nurse had transferred into his office. "Dr. Auckerman speaking."

"Sorry to disturb you this late in the afternoon, Dr. Auckerman. I'm Nurse

199

Martha Beckett. I worked in the geriatric department at Kingston General. I..." A door closed and the background noises died. "I learned you talk to my doctor on Friday."

Zachary had already seen all the patients with appointments. Her call didn't bother him or interrupt anything important, just some paperwork. "Good afternoon, Nurse Martha. I indeed called your department on Friday. I needed some information about a nurse who worked at the hospital. Your Doctor Crocker was most helpful."

"I doubt that." It sounded like she'd gagged on the words. "Dr. Crocker was only hired last spring. He's not a bad doctor, but... he kinda has a god complex. He likes his nurses to fade in the background, unless they're young, pretty... and female."

"Go on, Nurse Martha." Zachary wasn't naive. The image of an individual and its reflection behind closed doors didn't always align, regardless of his profession. "I'd like to hear what *you* have to say about Nurse Wiedrich."

"Darius was one of the best nurses I've ever worked with. He was highly qualified, kind, caring, and he went the extra ten miles for his patients. He even volunteered at a maximum-security penitentiary. The nursing staff adored him, all his patients loved him to pieces, even the ones locked up at Millhaven. I believe Dr. Crocker disliked Darius for these exact same reasons, not that Darius ever tried to outshine Dr. Crocker, at least not intentionally. Darius was just a great nurse who enjoyed reading to his patients if he wasn't busy. Dr. Crocker liked to call Darius's behavior unprofessional..." Her voice quivered. "Sorry but I still miss Darius. His death affected us all. When I heard you inquired about him, I felt the need to set his record straight. I owed him that much."

"I'm—" The word *death* registered Zachary's mind. "Dead? What do you mean by *his death*? Your doctor told me Darius quit his job in June."

"That part is true. He did quit in June. He was moving back to Calgary to be closer to his aging parents. He even had a job lined up at Rockyview General that was supposed to start in September..." She cleared her throat. "He died in a car crash on the Trans-Canada Highway near Regina. His poor parents, they never got a chance to... to say hello, or goodbye."

Stunned, Zachary sank in his armchair. "I'm sorry for your loss, Nurse Martha." All deaths were tragic, but some seemed more unjust than others. "Thank you for telling me about Nurse Darius. I wish I had the pleasure of meeting him." *Instead of his impostor.*

His door swung door. "We have an emergency, Dr. Zachary."

"I must go, Nurse Martha. Thanks again for your call."

* * *

Dirty and sore after spending most of her afternoon in crawl spaces, Willow enjoyed a long shower during which her mind wandered back to her conversation with Constable Laforge. *The male individual who broke the beaker is related to a felon named Fergus Lynch imprisoned at Millhaven.*

Except for Darius, all the male attendants had worked at the nursing home for years. If one of them had a relative serving a sentence for murder, the rumor would have spread around town like a brushfire. The only unknown character was Nurse Darius.

"The blood has to belong to Darius, does it not?"

The notion that an unknown individual without any ties to the nursing home, but related to a murderer in Millhaven, had managed to sneak in the basement, stumble on the lab, break a beaker, and leave without being seen was too ludicrous to even entertain.

"And where the heck is Millhaven?" Her curiosity piqued, she exited the shower and wrapped an oversized towel around her body. "Hey Siri, where is Millhaven Penitentiary?"

202

"Millhaven Institution is in Ontario," answered the digital smart aleck living inside her iPhone.

"I asked for penitentiary, not institution... never mind."

Without picking up her phone from the counter, Willow opened the browser and searched for Millhaven Penitentiary.

You were right, Siri. Millhaven Institution was a maximum-security prison in Bath, Ontario, not too far from Kingston.

"What's your connection to the felon serving time in Millhaven, Darius? Are you somehow related to that Fergus Lynch? Or did your DNA become mixed up with someone else?"

For a mix-up to have occurred, Darius would have had to visit the prison, but according to Constable Laforge, Fergus's only visitor was his elderly father.

"Are you related to a different inmate?" Another possibility occurred to Willow. "Or did you work at Millhaven?"

She dialed the institution, asked for the infirmary, and put the call on speaker.

"Infirmary. Edward speaking."

Droplets of water coursed down Willow's body. "Good afternoon, Edward. I'm..." A plumber wouldn't have any good reason to look for a nurse, but a doctor might. *Just keep it as truthful as possible so you don't contradict yourself.* "I'm Dr. Willow Mitchell. I'm trying to track down a nurse I worked with many years ago. His

203

name is Darius Wiedrich. He wouldn't work, or have worked, at Millhaven by any chance, would he?"

Rapid breathing disrupted the heavy silence at the other end. "I'm... I'm sorry to have to break the news to you, Doctor, but Darius died last July."

"He what?" If she'd held her phone, Willow would have dropped it. "What do you mean he's dead."

"Like in deceased..." Edward sounded as uncomfortable as Willow was confused. "I don't know what else to tell you. Darius volunteered at the infirmary two weekends a month for... for as long as I've worked here, and I've worked here five years. We last saw him at the end of June. He died a few weeks later in a car crash. Some inmates wept when they learned of his passing. That's how much he was liked around here."

Reeling from the information, Willow willed her voice to remain steady. "I... I was under the impression he was still alive. The Nurse Wiedrich I'm looking for is in his mid to late twenties, about six feet tall, thin, blond hair, fair skin, baby face." *And not liked much around here.*

Edward hiccupped a chuckle. "Wrong nurse, Doctor. Our Nurse Wiedrich was in his early forties, five feet nine, definitely not thin, dark buzz cut, neat beard, bronze complexion, and a nasty old scar across his cheek. He was like a giant teddy. Mean on the outside with a gentle soul in the inside."

204

Something buzzed on the line. "I have an incoming patient, Doctor. Sorry for scaring you."

He hung up and the screen of her phone went blank.

Unsure what she unearthed, but shuddering at the possibilities, Willow dialed Constable Laforge.

After four rings, Willow was redirected to a voicemail. "It's Willow Mitchell. Nurse Darius Wiedrich, the real nurse Wiedrich, may be deceased. Please call me back."

* * *

Too restless to wait for the constable's call, Willow drove to the hospital.

The doctor's SUV was parked in the last row even though plenty of unoccupied stalls were available closer to the entrance. He showed unselfish consideration toward his patients with limited mobility, and yet he played with her.

Still unable to reconcile the two facets of his conflicting personality, Willow scrutinized the lot for the silver car belonging to the pretty nurse.

For the sake of the nursing home residents, Willow was willing to set her feelings aside and talk to him, but she wasn't ready yet to face the pretty nurse.

No silver car. Good. Willow parked not too far from his SUV and hurried inside.

Less than a dozen individuals waited in the lobby. She returned a few acknowledgment nods heading to the nurses' station.

The woman whose compassion, work ethics, and integrity had earned her the top nursing position at the hospital set aside the file holding her attention and gazed into Willow's eyes, making her feel like the most important person in the hospital at this precise moment. "Hello, Mitch. What can I do for you?"

"I need to see the doctor, Angela. It's important. Very—" Heavy resounding steps prompted Willow to look over her shoulder.

The man she missed not talking to approached her.

"Willow?" A disarming smile lit up his face. "Do you have a minute? We need to talk." With a sweep of his arm, he invited her to follow him into his office, then closed the door behind him. "You need to be careful. I discovered Darius's name isn't Darius. He's impersonating a nurse who died in July. The real Nurse Darius worked in Kingston."

Stunned to hear her thoughts coming out of his mouth, Willow could only nod.

Edward was right. We weren't talking about the same nurse, except there was only one real Nurse Wiedrich, Edward's Nurse Wiedrich. Not mine. Understanding untied her tongue. "Constable Laforge called me,

206

Zachary. The blood on the bandage came from someone related to Fergus Lynch, a felon at the Millhaven Institution where the real Nurse Wiedrich volunteered his weekends."

"Lynch? They chanted Lynch when—" Knocks on the door interrupted Zachary. "Yes?"

Angela peeked her head inside his office. "Sorry for the intrusion, Doctor Zachary, but your landlord just arrived. He refuses to say what's wrong with him. He's in Exam Room One."

"I'll be right there." After dismissing his nurse, Zachary took Willow's hand into his and stroked her fingers. "I need to see Chester, but we need to finish that conversation. If it's okay, I'll stop by your place around seven this evening."

"Sure..." Dizzy from their exchange, Willow retrieved her hand to grip the top edge of his desk. Her gaze fell on a stack of old files. The names written in black marker on the tabs sticking out teased her memory. She blinked, and their significance struck her. These were all patients from the nursing home.

The door banged against the wall. Zachary had left it wide open after leaving the office.

Nana mentioned an Agnes. Unable to resist the opportunity to investigate another one of her grandmother's delusions, Willow browsed through the files. Halfway through, she stumbled onto Agnes Goose's file. *Let's see...*

While she was only interested in Agnes's room number, Willow inadvertently glanced over some personal details. Agnes, a nonagenarian suffering from severe hearing loss, poor vision, and dementia, lived on the main floor next to the service elevator.

The lab was dismantled in a few hours. Since the equipment couldn't have vanished into thin air, it had to have been moved somewhere. Somewhere near and inconspicuous, like a room on the main floor, easy to access from the basement.

A room like Agnes's.

* * *

From the doorway of Exam Room One, Zachary eyed the patient sitting on the exam bed.

"Chester, what a pleasure to see you." Tickled by the irony that the man who'd avoided him for weeks sought his services, Zachary stepped in and closed the door. "Did you come to waive the penalty if I break the lease?"

His patient's nostrils flared. "I don't like being threatened by a lawsuit, *Doctor*."

"I'll let you in on a little secret, Chester. I don't like being lied to, I hate mice, and I can't stand people who abuse workers by not paying them their fair dues, so..." Immune to his patient's outburst, Zachary sat on a swivel stool and rolled to the foot of the bed. "What brings you here?"

Chester glared at him. "I need a doctor. Will you deny me care if I don't cave in?"

Upon his graduation from medical school, Zachary had sworn an oath, an oath he'd never broken. "Of course not, that would be unethical and unprofessional." *Not that I expect you to know the definition of these words.*

"Don't give me that moral bullshit." His patient spat in the garbage can by the bed, further annoying Zachary. "I'm not the one sleeping with two women."

The accusation flew so high over his head, Zachary didn't feel the breeze. "What women?"

"Your nurse and your plumber. They made a public display of their confrontation." His soon-to-be ex-landlord sneered. "I should be charging you more for entertaining guests and suing you for extortion. The money I owed Mitch was none of your business."

Chester's acknowledgement that he didn't pay his debt to Willow registered in Zachary's mind, but he drew a blank at the accusations. If any rumors circulated about him having an affair with a woman, let alone two, they hadn't burned his ears yet. He couldn't fathom how Chester concluded that

Zachary was also involved with one of his nurses. "What nurse?"

"Are you taking me for an idiot?" Chester fumbled with his phone then shoved it in front of Zachary's eyes. "She's half-naked in the doorway."

Thunderstruck by Nurse Camille's appearance, Zachary grabbed the phone and enlarged the picture. The coy smile curling his nurse's lips was as unmistakable as the shock on Willow's face. "When did you take that photo?"

"Last week, early Monday morning." His sleazy landlord snatched his phone back. "There's mouse traps in the shed. I was going to get them and put them under the trailer, but I decided not to intrude. If you gave them keys, I expect them back."

Keys... As Zachary recalled the strange events that had marked not only last Monday but the entire week, he fought to contain his outrage. "I'd like you to message me that photo. Now if you please. You still have my number, don't you?" *Even though you're not returning my calls.*

His patient swiped his thumb across the screen of his phone. "I'm warning you, I'm not deleting it."

If Chester believed he could use the photo to blackmail Zachary, the man faced a rude awakening. "You can frame it for all I care." A few seconds later, his phone vibrated in the pocket of his lab coat.

Zachary checked it. "Got it. Thank you. So, what brings you here if not the lawsuit?"

"It's... it's the old chap." Chester cupped the front of his sweatpants, his antagonistic attitude crumbling into obvious discomfiture. "I think I broke it."

Chapter 12

Willow pulled into the parking lot of the nursing home. The director's monstrous green Hummer was nowhere to be seen, but Darius's red convertible was parked near the side entrance.

The clock on her dashboard indicated 5:23 p.m.

Dinner starts at 5 pm and lasts ninety minutes. Her timing was perfect. Residents and staff alike would be in the dining room. Willow shouldn't encounter anyone in the corridors.

She entered the building by the front entrance and strolled by Elisabeth's office. The door was ajar. Perplexed, Willow paused in front of it.

The director had never struck her as the type of woman who would give anyone the opportunity to sneak into her office during her absence, not with the number of confidential documents she kept of the residents and employees.

Thinking she might be wrong to assume Elisabeth wasn't on premises even though her Hummer wasn't in the parking lot, Willow knocked. "Elisabeth?"

The door opened on its own. The lights were on, but the office wasn't occupied.

Willow stepped in.

A four-drawer file cabinet stood next to the window. Labels were affixed to the drawers, daring her to solve the mystery of Darius's identity.

In front of the lower drawer labeled *Employees* sat a pair of low heel black pumps. Willow squatted to set the footwear aside so she could open the drawer. The pumps toppled sideways, their heels facing each other. From her vantage point, the toe box of one appeared larger than the other's.

Baffled by the optical illusion, Willow took a closer look at the shoes she assumed belonged to Elisabeth. Size 9 and size 9W were stamped in faded black ink on the beige soles soiled with dark toe imprints.

The difference in width registered at the same time than the unusual configurations of the toe imprints in the left pump.

"What are you doing?" bellowed a deep voice.

Willow's heart rate spiked. She dropped the shoes and jumped to her feet.

"I will ask again." From the doorway, Darius eyed her like a hawk in hunting mode. "Why are you here?"

"The... the door opened when I knocked." Rattled by her discovery, Willow struggled to come up with a valid excuse for trespassing. *Darius should have been in the dining room... No, not Darius.* His real name wasn't Darius. *The real Darius is dead.*

Zachary's warning came back to haunt her. In the blink of an eye, the precariousness of her situation sank in, playing further havoc with her heart rate.

Don't panic. Keep it together and plausible. "I... I wanted to talk to Elisabeth about the lock on Nana's door." Her indignation and annoyance rose to the surface. "Whose idea was it to rob my grandmother of her privacy and freedom by removing the inside latch and locking her in at night? Yours or Elisabeth's?"

The fake Darius's expression grew darker, more impenetrable. "We meant well, but I'll relay your objections to Elisabeth, and we'll correct the situation tonight. Is there anything else I can help you with?"

Fearing that he might be eager to get rid of her in every sense of the word, Willow shook her head and left the building. Once she unlocked her van, she remembered the real reason behind her visit.

She had to go back in to check on Agnes, but not until Fake Darius's shift was over.

* * *

An emergency shortly before seven played havoc with Zachary's evening plan.

He sent a quick text to Willow while Nurse Heather wheeled a boy in Exam Room Two.

Emergency. See you between 8 - 9 pm. Zachary

The eleven-year-old boy suffered scratches on his face trying to save his small dog from being taken by a coyote.

The coyote wasn't captured, and therefore couldn't be tested for rabies. Since there was a slim chance the wild animal was infected and able to transmit the virus, Zachary had no choice but to administer rabies immune globulin into the wounds and give the boy his first vaccine.

"We're done, Dylan. You were very brave." Zachary turned toward the boy's mother. "Nurse Heather will explain how to take care of the wounds and when to return for his next rabies vaccine. If you're worried about anything, do not hesitate to come back."

Angela entered the exam room. "Once you're done here, Doctor, we have another emergency."

Confident he would still be able to leave the hospital before nine o'clock, Zachary refrained from sending Willow another text.

* * *

Parked in the street, in the shadow of an evergreen laden with snow, Willow enjoyed a clear view of the front entrance and the parking lot of the nursing home.

She couldn't afford to run into Fake Darius twice in the same evening and risk raising his suspicion. Therefore, before entering Agnes's room, Willow had to wait for him to leave the premises.

Fortunately, the text she received from Zachary gave her an extra hour to investigate.

Around seven o'clock, Fake Darius exited the building then zoomed out of the parking lot in his red convertible, showing total disregard for the speed limit.

Irked by his inconsiderate behavior, Willow dug her fingernails into her steering wheel. A tall snowbank hid the side door in front of which some able-bodied residents huddled for a smoke in the evening or at night. Someone driving too fast along the building could accidently clip a resident without even realizing it.

No residents stood in the cold tonight, but from Nana's bedroom window, Willow had often glanced at their silhouettes and the orange tips of their cigarettes.

Come to think of it, I haven't seen the sweet old lady with a beaver hat in weeks, not since the second suspicious death...

A chilling thought crossed Willow's mind. She didn't know the name of the old lady, but the timing of her disappearance fit with the death of the second victim. The one with possible frostbite.

What if the old lady took off her right glove to light her cigarette? What if she was hit by a car, and not a snowmobile? What if she wasn't found until hours later?

Willow's theory contained lots of *ifs*, but it explained the victim's frozen fingertips.

I need to talk to Nana.

Willow tried using her grandmother's key to enter by the side door and was shocked to discover the door was unlocked. Anyone could sneak in or out undetected, forgetful residents and suspicious strangers alike.

Once again, Willow was surprised by Elisabeth's lack of concern for the residents' safety. *Why am I concerned? There's already a suspicious impostor on the premises and his job is to take care of the residents.*

Willow marched down the deserted corridor. Around the corner, something entered her peripheral vision. She sidestepped, avoiding a collision with her grandmother at the last second.

"Nana? What are you doing wandering on the main floor alone at night?" A possible and scary explanation dawned on Willow. *I played right into Fake Darius's hands when I objected to Nana being locked in her room.*

Should her grandmother wander somewhere unsafe and suffer an accident, neither Fake Darius nor Elisabeth would be responsible since the directive came from the victim's granddaughter.

Despite her late husband's many faults, he hadn't deserved to die alone in a pond. Willow didn't wish that kind of death on anyone, but she was ready to make an exception for the cunning impostor. *Someone needs to take you hunting, Darius, or whatever your real name is.*

She steered Nana toward the elevator, up a floor, and into her room. Her grandmother's nightgown was damp with sweat. Willow helped her don a clean one. "Nana, do you remember the lady who was hit by a snowmobile?"

"I can button my nighty alone." She swatted Willow's hand away, and with frail and shaky fingers, attempted to slide the small button into the hole. "I'm not an invalid and I'm tired of living with cranky old people."

You're a cranky old lady, Nana. Trust me, I feel your pain. Willow bit her tongue waiting for the button to go in or for her grandmother to give up.

After a few minutes, Nana slipped the button into the wrong hole. "See, I don't need help, and I didn't imagine the snowmobile. It was red."

Willow's heart rate accelerated faster than a sports car. The only red car she'd ever spotted in the parking lot of the nursing home belonged to Darius. "What about the lady, Nana? Was she smoking? Did she wear a hat?"

Her grandmother slumped in her bed before she could button the rest of her nightgown. "A beaver was sleeping on her head. Can I have a smoke?"

A forlorn sigh whished through Willow's teeth. "You don't smoke, Nana. Good night. And please, don't get up."

"The cute boy fixed my door." Her grandmother's lower lip jutted out in a sulky pout. "He said I could go anywhere I wanted."

Of course he did. "No, you cannot go anywhere. Good night, Nana."

Once Nana fell asleep, Willow headed for Agnes's room.

* * *

Hoping to avoid an abdominal surgery, Zachary proceeded with the insertion of a nasogastric tube before admitting his latest patient for the night.

With any luck, the partial intestinal obstruction would clear on its own.

In the meantime, Zachary trusted Nurse Heather to monitor the patient. "Call me immediately if there's any sudden changes to his condition."

On his way out of the hospital, he checked his watch. 8:32. "Good. I technically have 28 minutes to shower and put on a fresh set of clothes before I'm late for real."

He jumped into his SUV and took the shortcut by the church. A red car, partially hidden in the church parking lot, caught his attention. Having seen too much blood in his life, Zachary hated that color with a passion. He would never drive a red vehicle, or wear a red shirt, or paint a fence red, or—

A furtive shadow moved along the snowbank.

Thinking he might have spotted the coyote that attacked the boy, Zachary slowed on the snow-covered back alley.

As the shadow approached the red car, it grew taller until it no longer crouched but stood like a human being. The individual stepped into the car then lay low on the front seat, but for a few seconds, the interior light illuminated his face.

"Darius?" *No, not Darius.* His real name didn't matter at the moment, but his covert presence around the church raised Zachary's suspicion. "Are you conducting drug deals in the church parking lot?"

Seconds later, Zachary pulled into his driveway then entered his trailer. In the kitchen, three mice nibbled on the table where a bowl of sugar was tipped sideways, spilling most of its contents on a blue mat.

His aggravation, exacerbated by the uncontrollable events in his and Willow's lives, reached an intolerable high. Zachary elbowed the table. Scared off, the mice scampered on the floor. "Where did Chester say he kept the moose traps? In the shed?"

Zachary marched out the back door and trudged through the snow, his blood pressure rising with every heavy breath he expelled in the cold air. Once he reached the dented aluminum shed, he kicked the padlock latch open. His phone provided the light he needed to search for the traps among the clutter.

A wheelbarrow missing its front tire and a wooden toboggan blocked his path. Zachary shoved the items by the door, then crawled behind them. Tires were stacked in the corner, and next to them were—

A deafening explosion rang in his ears and threw him onto the tires where he crumbled on the floor. The shed crashed onto him, smacking his lights out.

* * *

Wiggling two picks into a keyhole to unlock a door looked easier in the movies than in real life. After ten minutes, Willow gave up. *A good burglar, I am not.*

A door creaked farther down the corridor from Agnes's room. Afraid to be caught breaking in, Willow retreated to the staircase but kept the fire door ajar so she could peek.

An elderly man in his birthday suit headed toward her, jiggling more than the keys in his hand. He stopped in front of the door of Agnes's neighbor, then unlocked it using a key.

Stunned by the surreal scene, Willow gaped, but then she remembered a conversation with Elisabeth regarding her grandmother's sex life. The director had said something about most keys opening most doors.

Once the man disappeared inside the room, Willow marched back to Agnes's then inserted Nana's key into the keyhole and turned.

A faint click reached Willow's ears, and the door opened. Less than impressed that any residents could access anyone else's room, Willow stepped into Agnes's.

The blinds weren't drawn. Lights from the lampposts cast a white glow on the heavy woman lying motionless in bed.

"Agnes?"

The elderly lady's breathing was shallow and raspy. Willow checked her pulse at the wrist. It was slow and steady, but Agnes's skin was clammy to the touch.

"What happened to you? Did someone drug you?"

Hoping to rouse Agnes with a cold facecloth, Willow entered the bathroom, switched the light on, and froze. The tub was filled with empty beakers, tubes, pipes, and everything else she'd seen in the basement.

"Nana was right." Somehow the rumor mills had blown the information into her grandmother's ear.

Out of desperation, Willow called Zachary. She might not trust him with her heart, but right now, she trusted him with her life.

It rang once. Twice. Three times. *Come on, Doc. Answer.*

His voicemail kicked in after the fourth ring. "You've reached Dr. Zachary Auckerman. Please leave a message, I will get back to you as soon as possible."

Willow swallowed the words eager to escape her mouth and waited for the beep before speaking.

"Zachary, it's Willow. Where are you? I found the drug lab, what's left of it. It's in Agnes Goose's bathroom. Her room is on the main floor, near the service elevator. Agnes is in bed, but she isn't responsive. I think she may have been drugged. My money is on Darius, the fake Darius. I think he also ran over Georgia with his car while she smoked in the parking lot, leaving her to die in the cold. Nana said it was a red snowmobile. His car is red. It would explain the frostbite on her fingers." Willow couldn't rule out Fake Darius's involvement in any of the suspicious deaths. "He caught me snooping in Elisabeth's office. I looked at her shoes. One was wider than the other. The toe imprints inside the wider one were smudged, but I'm pretty sure I counted six. I

223

think she's my paternal aunt, the one who killed my mother. I'm going home."

She turned the bathroom lights off and returned into the room. The elderly lady hadn't moved a muscle.

Willow debated taking Agnes with her, but she doubted she'd be able to carry Agnes's dead weight all the way to her van. "I'll come back with the doctor, Agnes. I promise."

Eager to escape the nursing home, Willow marched to the door. It was ajar.

I closed the door. I know I closed it when I came in.

A wave of panic swept her off her feet then something stung her neck. She jerked backward and hit a soft wall of flesh.

Her scream died on her lips.

* * *

Roused from a nightmarish dream, Zachary slowly opened his eyes. Sirens blared in the distance. The noise pierced the foggy layers of his mind, triggering a massive headache. *What on earth happened?*

A light filtered through the darkness enveloping him. He reached for it and stumbled on his phone, still in flashlight mode.

Memories of the last minutes... hours... flashed in front of his eyes.

It wasn't a dream. He'd lost the notion of time, but he was certain he didn't imagine the explosion or the presence of the impostor in the parking lot of the church, meters away from his trailer.

The trailer? Zachary peeked through the rubble of the shed in which he was buried. Flames rose from the ground where the trailer once stood. *That wasn't how I'd planned to solve my rodent infestation, but that worked.* The lame joke served to dissipate the tension coiling his insides.

Had he not looked for the traps in the shed, he would be dead. The mice had saved his life. He would laugh at the irony if not for the suspicion that the impostor's presence in the vicinity was somehow linked in the explosion.

The sirens died and a firetruck parked nearby, its red lights flashing in the night.

Zachary inhaled sharply, but his scream for help died in his throat at the last second. *If I am right about the impostor intentionally blowing up my trailer, he will either flee or try to kill me again once he realizes his first attempt failed. Either way, it could be in my best interest to remain missing, or presumed dead, until I share my suspicion with the authorities.*

Hoping to escape the shed without being seen by anyone, friends or foes, Zachary shone his light around looking for an opening. Through a gap between the wheelbarrow and an aluminum ladder, he spied his neighbor's garage.

The opening didn't look large enough, but he didn't have anything to lose by trying to crawl through. At worst the ladder would collapse, he would get stuck and be forced to call for help.

Here goes nothing...

He moved his left leg then his right. Neither felt broken nor pinned down. Cautious not to dislodge anything that might hit him or trap him, he squeezed his body between the wheelbarrow and the ladder. Something dug into his right thigh, tearing his scrubs and scraping his skin.

He sucked in a shaky breath, then heedless of the searing pain traveling up his leg, he pushed forward. The smell of charred metal and burning debris assailed his nose. He peeked his head into the night then writhed his right shoulder out. A low rumble reverberated around him.

Fearing an imminent cave-in, he dug one elbow into the snow, and using it as lever, he cleared his other shoulder. Something screeched. Fueled by desperation, Zachary hauled his lower body out.

The rubble rumbled.

"Anyone there?" The noise had attracted the attention of a firefighter. "Anyone needing help?"

Crouched down, with one finger pressed against the light of his phone to dim it, Zachary trudged through the snow until he reached his neighbor's garage. Once out of view, he used the wall as support to stand. His legs hurt, and a warm substance trickled down his right one.

He turned off the flashlight. *Missed call* and *voicemail* appeared on his screen. Willow had called him around the time of the explosion. Relieved to hear from her, he listened to her voicemail.

The information she conveyed deadened the pain in his leg and chased away the fatigue in his body, replacing them with a renewed sense of urgency.

Stay home, Willow. I'm coming as fast as I can.

* * *

Willow awoke with a funny taste lingering in her mouth and a musky odor assaulting her nose. Memories of the attack resurfaced. She fought the terror paralyzing her, a terror amplified by the darkness surrounding her.

Take a deep breath. You're not dead. Not yet.

Listening to the crazy voice teetering on the edge of sanity inside her skull, she breathed in and out until she could no longer hear the thumping of her heart. Between two erratic breaths, she became aware nothing obstructed her mouth. Whoever drugged her—

No, not whoever. In Agnes's room, Willow had tumbled backward into someone's soft bosoms. *Elisabeth?*

The urge to scream swelled inside Willow, but she didn't waste her energy. If there was a chance anyone could hear her, she would have been gagged, not just drugged.

Her buttocks hurt from sitting on a hard surface. She straightened her back, only to grimace in pain. Her spine pushed back against a protruding pipe. She shifted her weight sideways but failed to relieve the pressure on her bruised spine. Her legs were bound at the ankles and her hands tied to the pipe.

She stretched her fingers to feel her bindings. A nylon rope encircled her wrists. She scratched the gritty pipe searching for the knot, and winced. The surface of the pipe had scraped a layer of skin off her fingers but given her an idea.

Hoping to fray the nylon rope, she contorted her upper body, and twisting her wrists back and forth, she rubbed the rope against the pipe.

A light coming from the corridor pierced the darkness, illuminating the room in which she was trapped, a room in which she'd spent too much time recently. The boiler room.

Feeling fuzz on the rope, she pulled. It scorched her wrists without breaking. *I need more time.*

Steps resounded in the basement, the sound intensifying with every thump. Hoping to be left alone if she showed no signs of having regained consciousness, she slumped back against the pipe and closed her eyes.

The darkness enhanced her other senses.

A faint smell tickled her nose. Someone had entered the boiler room, the scent of cheap cologne betraying his presence.

A switch clicked and a red veil fell over her eyelids.

"You're twitching, Mitch." The lack of emotion in Fake Darius's voice stirred the fear bottled up in the pit of her stomach. "If you're awake, I suggest you open your eyes, or else I'll be forced to wake you with an injection."

While she disliked the idea of surrendering to his menace, she didn't want anyone to stick another needle anywhere in her body.

She peered at him through narrowed eyes. "Elisabeth was the one who caught me in Agnes's room, and yet, here you are. You make quite a pair, you know." *Keep talking.* Sooner or later, Zachary would listen to her message and wonder what happened to her. She needed to buy him time to rescue her. "Was it an accident when you ran over

Georgia, the elderly lady smoking in the parking lot, or did you intend to kill her? What about the other lady, the one whose head was stuck between her mattress and box spring? Was it also an accident or did you smother her? And the man who drowned in his bath? Or Alphonse? You and Elisabeth like poking people in the neck, don't you?"

His arms crossed over his chest, Fake Darius stared at her with an expression she couldn't decipher. "You're cleverer than I gave you credit for, Mitch. Just to set the record straight, not that it matters really, running over the old lady was an accident. I wish I'd avoided her. You should have seen the dent she made on my car. It cost me almost two thousand bucks to get it fixed."

A wave of nausea flooded Willow's stomach. To hear him feel sorry about his car, and not his victim, disgusted her. *I'm glad your mechanic overcharged you.*

"I also didn't smother the grumpy old rag, but her nephew did. He paid me five thousand dollars to make it look like an accident. I started working in this rat hole because I had to lay low for a while, but Elisabeth isn't paying me that well. I would have been an idiot to say no to some extra cash. Now, you're wrong about Pete. He ventured in the basement while I was brewing an experimental potion. He's the one who insisted to taste it. I didn't shove it down his throat. When he didn't die right away, I took him back to his room." Fake

Darius's lack of remorse and disregard for human life was chilling. "I found him hours later in his bath, on the brink of death. It was only a matter of minutes before he slid under the water and drowned. I wanted to help along, but that would have been murder. Despite what you might think, I'm not a cold-blooded murderer. So, I waited."

The semantic distinction between drowning someone and letting someone drown flew over her head. Hours had elapsed between the time that Peter Tanguay had ingested the deadly brew and the time he drowned, hours during which Nana had heard about the brew, hours during which Fake Darius could have sought medical help, but didn't. "What about Alphonse Morrison? Did you give him the syringe so he could stab himself in the neck?"

"It was self-defense. Unlike the rest of the bunch, Morrison wasn't senile, but he was noisy. Too noisy. I couldn't let him poke his nose in my business, but like you, he wasn't easily intimidated." Fake Darius shrugged. "He got what he deserved. And so will you. Elisabeth was careless to grant you access to the basement while I conducted my experiments, but you only have yourself to blame for snooping around." His face darkened. "We both underestimated you and your doctor. He's dead by the way. I blew up his trailer—with him in it."

It took a few seconds for the words to sink in, for Willow's world to collapse. "You're lying."

"Am I?" The killer approached her, waggling his phone. "Would you like to watch his demise? Of course you do." A ruthless sneer tugged at his lips. Fake Darius accessed his screen, then moments later held the phone in front of her eyes. "Watch."

For a few seconds, the image remained still, but then Zachary's SUV pulled into his driveway beside Chester's trailer. The lamppost illuminated Zachary's unmistakable silhouette. He entered his home. The screen froze on the trailer, its focus on the door, the same door where Camille had stood wrapped in a towel.

Willow's mind took a sharp and unexpected turn down memory lane. *Why was Camille still wrapped in a towel?*

According to the pretty nurse, Zachary had run out of hot water because she used it all, but when Willow showed up at the trailer, he'd already left. If Camille had truly taken her shower first, shouldn't she also have had time to get dressed for work? Her silver car was in his driveway. Heat had emanated from the hood, but the engine wasn't running. *The car wasn't warming up, it was cooling down.* The inconsistency in Camille's story dawned on Willow at the same the trailer vanished in a thunderous explosion.

Zachary? Nooooo! A schism split open the floor of the basement, swallowing Willow's heart and soul. She never gave him a chance to explain, and now he was gone. It was too late. She'd lost everything.

"It was his fault, and yours." The killer pocketed his phone. "He shouldn't have interrogated Henry, Elisabeth's clerk, about her late husband's death. And you, *Doctor Mitchell*, shouldn't have called the prison to inquire about the real Nurse Darius Wiedrich. Edward, the nurse you talked to at the infirmary, is a blabbermouth. He thought the mix-up was funny, so he recounted your call to my dad, except my dad didn't laugh. He warned me about you."

"You're Fergus Lynch's son?" Her hatred for Lynch Junior stirred the ashes of her life, breeding a singular emotion, an overwhelming feeling that spread to every fiber of her being. Revenge. "You'll rot in jail, just like him."

"Sorry to disappoint you, but I have other plans. Unfortunately, I've been instructed not to *harm* you. At least not yet. Feel free to cry and mourn your doctor. I'll come back to check on you later, after I lure your grandmother into the kitchen since you forbade me to lock her in her room. I bet you didn't know she likes to play with matches, did you?"

Chapter 13

Plunged once again into darkness, Willow renewed her grinding effort to wear out the rope.

You missed your last chance to kill me, Lynch Junior. You and Elisabeth will pay for your crimes. I will hunt you down and—

The rope snapped, freeing her hands. Without wasting any time massaging her sore wrists, Willow tackled the rope around her ankles, but quickly realized it wasn't a rope but a thick zip tag, the kind used to secure the exhaust duct of a dryer. She probed the cubic head.

Really? Astounded by their carelessness or overconfidence, she pressed the tab. The reusable zip tag loosened around her ankles then came off when she spread her feet apart. *I can't believe you or Elisabeth used a reusable tie to secure my legs.*

The boiler room held no secrets, not after the many times she serviced the darn thing, so Willow marched right out in the dark. Once in the corridor, she turned the light on then searched for a weapon. In one of the rooms she stumbled on a steel pipe about the length of a baseball bat.

For a moment, she considered climbing the condemned staircase instead of riding the noisy elevator, but the moment passed. Gaining the element of surprise would have been nice, but not at the risk of being trapped underneath a pile of rotten beams and studs.

She turned all the lights off, pressed the calling button of the elevator then took position against the wall, ready to swing at anyone coming out.

The cables rattled, the door squeaked open, and the interior light of the cage spilled into the corridor. Inhaling and exhaling slowly, she counted to three. When no one exited, she peeked inside. It was empty.

Grateful for the reprieve, Willow stepped in.

The service elevator only ran back and forth between the basement and the main floor. A quieter elevator provided a smoother ride between the main and second floor.

Willow retreated into the corner of the service elevator, near the control panel, ready to fight her way out. Her heartrate and breathing didn't increase. She felt no fear, no panic, no exhilaration. Something had died inside her, numbing her body but strengthening her desire for vengeance.

The elevator came to an abrupt stop and the door slid open.

She raised the pipe and strained her ears

for any footsteps, any chatter, any sounds associated with a human being. Hearing none, she risked a glance.

The long corridor was deserted.

* * *

Alone in Willow's kitchen, Zachary called Constable Laforge, catching her on her way to work.

Drawing strength and composure from his medical training, he recounted the latest events in a coherent manner.

"Willow should have come home by now, Constable. If the impostor posing as Darius tried to kill me, he may have targeted Willow next." Dark scenarios entered Zachary's mind, threatening to unleash the emotions he struggled hard to contain. "I need help."

"Take a deep breath, Doc. I just signaled for reinforcement and I'm heading your way. We'll have officers in Ojibson in about an hour. In the meantime, I want you to stay in Willow's house in case she returns. This impostor is a dangerous man. Please, don't give him the chance to successfully eliminate you. Let us handle the situation."

Despondent and powerless to help, Zachary slumped in a chair. A draft of cold air prickled his face, threatening to invade his heart. He looked at the back door. The weatherstripping was damaged, undoubtedly as a result of his forced entry.

I promise to get it fixed, Willow.

His gaze traveled from the door to the red droplets tracing his path through the kitchen then settled on his bloody pant scrub. At the sight of the long bleeding laceration on his thigh, his medical training kicked in once more, dispersing the dark cloud hovering over his head.

In case of a severe emergency, the fate of the patient often depended on a timely intervention. Every single minute counted.

Willow's life is in danger. I can't wait an hour for the RCMP to arrive. He tightly wrapped two tea towels around his thigh to stop the bleeding, but in his condition, it would take him half an hour to walk to the hospital. *I need a ride. Now.*

Zachary went to knock on the neighbor's door.

* * *

Willow hurried down the corridor toward the dining room.

If Lynch Junior hasn't dragged Nana in the kitchen yet, he will soon. I might as well wait for them there.

Along the way, she pulled a fire alarm. The shrill sound of the alarm rang in her ears. Doors were slammed open or shut, and steps pounded the corridors. She urged the residents she encountered to exit the building.

Upon entering dining room, Willow paused among the tables set for breakfast. No one occupied the chairs yet, but the door leading to the kitchen was ajar.

Amid the noisy alarm, a scream wafted into the dining room.

Nana? Adrenaline flooded Willow's bloodstream. She inched toward the kitchen door and pushed it with her elbow. Ready to strike, she peeked inside.

Caught between the sink and the stove, seemingly unaware of her entrance, Lynch Junior attempted to take away her grandmother's walker, but Nana's tight grip on the handles resisted his efforts.

Impressed by her grandmother's remarkable resilience, Willow approached him from behind and took a swing with the pipe. "Let her go."

The pipe connected with his hip bone.

A guttural scream rose in the air. Lynch Junior pushed her grandmother, and they both tumbled onto the floor amid Nana's shrieking.

"Nana!"

Her grandmother slumped motionless over her twisted walker.

Next to her, his face contorted in a hideous grimace, Lynch Junior clutched his side in obvious pain. "You?"

"Move a muscle, Lynch, and I'll bash your nose into your brain." The residual vibrations from the pipe reverberated through Willow's arms, intensifying the inexplicable tremors shaking her body. "Nana? Can you hear me?"

"You killed her with your little stunt." Lynch Junior sneered at her. "Thanks to you, she's dead."

"Shut up, Lynch." Ready to silence him with another blow, Willow knelt next to her grandmother and took her pulse.

"You're going to pay for this, Mitchell." Lynch Junior attempted to stand only to collapse on the floor once more.

"Hang in there, Nana." The flutter of Nana's eyelashes heartened Willow. "I'm calling for help."

Her grandmother required immediate medical assistance, and so did the man sprawled on the floor, but Willow couldn't bring herself to care about his fate.

She reached into her pocket for her phone. A sudden jab in her shoulder sent her spiraling down into oblivion.

* * *

Zachary directed Willow's neighbor to stop by the east side entrance of the hospital. "Thanks again for the ride, Mr. Alexander."

"Any time, Doc, and don't worry, I won't mention it to anyone." The retired truck driver switched gear to P. "Take good take care of that leg. We need you in one piece."

The town people might need him, but the neighbor's readiness to help reminded Zachary that he could also count on them in moment of dire need. He belonged in Ojibson and he'd be damned if he let a few rotten apples destroy his future by harming the woman he loved.

A sign on the door stopped Zachary in his tracks.

No Entry - Staff Only
All visitors must use main
entrance

He'd only exited through this door, never used it to enter, and never paid much attention to the keypad. Hoping the six-digit code he'd memorized on his arrival hadn't changed, he entered it on the keypad and tried the handle.

To his relief, the door swung open. He ventured into the quiet east wing and entered the morgue.

Blood hadn't seeped through the tea towels wrapped around his leg. The bleeding appeared under control, and he was up to date in his tetanus shots, but the wound still demanded his attention before he began searching for Willow.

He unwrapped the makeshift bandage. Now that it'd stopped bleeding actively, the wound proved to be not as deep as he'd feared. He quickly closed the laceration with three stitches done at more or less equal intervals then applied butterfly bandages in-between sutures without caring about the appearance of the scar that would mar his thigh after it healed.

Once done, he accessed Elisabeth Brown's medical records from the lab computer. Willow suspected Elisabeth of having six toes, a fact he wanted to confirm before confronting her and her deceitful nurse.

He couldn't afford to waste time chasing after the wrong person. "Let's see..."

Elisabeth's last medical visit preceded Holloway's death. The routine checkup didn't reveal anything interesting, so Zachary browsed through her previous visits.

Every May, for as long as her records showed, she visited Holloway for her annual checkup, but Elisabeth hadn't seen any of the visiting doctors who had sporadically come and gone over the last four years.

Zachary would have expected otherwise from a patient who obviously took care of her health. "Are you hiding something? Or do you just dislike visiting doctors?"

From years to years, the checkups were the same and yielded similar results. Nothing stood out until the mention of a toenail fungal infection during a December appointment twelve years ago.

Abscess between 4th and

little toe. Drained. Nail fungus on lil little toe. Possible bacterial and fungal infection. Oral and topical antibio—

Zachary did a double take on the infected toe. "Lil little toe? Is that a typo, Holloway, or did you mean second little toe?"

Suspecting the latest, he memorized the address in her records then rushed out of the morgue. With any luck, one of his nurses would let him borrow her vehicle. Around the corner, he bumped into Angela.

"Doc?" Rooted on the spot, she stared at him with widening eyes. "You're... you're alive." Her stupor quickly faded. "You have no idea how glad I am to see you." She grabbed his arm. "The nursing home is on fire. The firefighters found Willow's grandmother and Nurse Darius unresponsive on the kitchen floor. They just brought them in."

* * *

Willow pushed through the layers of confusion entrapping her mind and blinked away the psychedelic images swirling in front of her eyes.

A long stainless-steel table appeared in her field of vision. A surgical lamp set to low hovered above it and medical instruments lay on a shelf underneath it. The chamber somewhat resembled an operating room.

Where am I?

The memories of her fight with Lynch Junior flooded back into her mind. She'd incapacitated him before he could set the kitchen on fire, but someone had poked her. Again.

I'm beginning to seriously hate needles.

A shadow glided down the staircase. "What am I going to do with you?"

Startled by the coldness in Elisabeth's voice, Willow recoiled in her chair. It wobbled unsteadily. For a few erratic heartbeats, she feared she would tumble, but then she regained her balance by the tips of her boots. The realization that her wrists and ankles were strapped to the chair struck her at the same time her location did. The embalmment room in Elisabeth's funeral home.

Willow never imagined she would be detained in this room while she was still alive.

"I see you've regained your senses." Elisabeth stepped out of the shadow, stopping near the table. "You made a mistake moving back to Ojibson, Mitch. You should have let me take care of your grandmother instead of poking your nose where it didn't belong."

For once, I totally agree with you. "Are you going to kill me like you—" Before making accusations, she glanced at Elisabeth's brown loafers. From her vantage point, Willow couldn't swear one shoe was larger than the other one, but she didn't dream the sole imprints in the black pumps that Elisabeth kept in her office. "Like you killed my mother?"

Elisabeth shrugged off the accusation. "I didn't kill Brigitte, at least not intentionally, but I did fantasize wringing Cedric's neck. Trust me, hiring the little prick wasn't my idea. If I hadn't had a debt to pay to his father, I would have notified the Mounties the moment I found his chemistry set." The admission shed a light on Lynch Junior's real name but not on Brigitte's death. "I should thank you for incapacitating him. Now Cedric will die in a fire of his own making."

"Glad to be of service. That's what family is for, isn't it? Did you know that a female relative on my father's side fought with my mother before she died?" Willow held her likely aunt's heated gaze. "The police found *your* DNA under my mother's fingernails, Elisabeth, or should I say Auntie Lizzie with six toes?"

"Wow, Mitch, I'm impressed you found out. I can count on one hand, a normal hand, how many people know about my extra toe. My late husband wasn't even one of them. He thought I was sleeping with socks because my feet were always cold." Lit up by a smug smile, Elisabeth's expression

244

softened. "There might be more Drewer blood flowing in those veins of yours than Mitchell's, but which one is thicker?"

The question didn't sound rhetorical. If anything, it implied Elisabeth might be hesitant to dispose of a blood relative.

Hoping she didn't misread between the lines, Willow feigned a more conciliatory attitude. "My mother never cared about me. As far as I'm concerned, she got what she deserved, but I'm curious to learn how you *unintentionally* stabbed her. Or did you entrust the task to Cedric?"

"Cedric?" Elisabeth sneered at the suggestion. "The arrogant little prick couldn't even silence you. Your mother would have eaten him alive. Literally. Do you realize I drove all night to make it to Ottawa before breakfast? Before Brigitte set her destructive scheme in motion? By the time I knocked on her door, I was tired, hungry, and cranky. I tried to reason with her, you know. I begged her not to ruin Doug's reputation, but she wouldn't listen. We fought. There was a pair of scissors on a table. I grabbed them. She tried to wrestle them from me... Next thing I know, she collapsed on the floor, gasping. When I saw the scissors poking from her chest and blood seeping through her nightgown, I knew she was beyond saving. I'm a compassionate woman, Mitch. I couldn't let Brigitte suffer, that would have been cruel, so I helped her pull out the scissors before I fled. I find it

245

comforting to know she died quickly, almost painlessly—don't you?"

No, I don't. Her aunt's twisted concept of mercy killing nauseated Willow. "Didn't you realize she scratched you while you fought?"

"Not until I was in my car. By then it was too risky to go back." Elisabeth began pacing the chamber. "Maybe I should turn myself in and tell the police that Brigitte threatened me... we fought... Both our prints are on the scissors. The police can't prove who held the scissors when she was stabbed. Good thing I didn't think of erasing my prints. It would have made me look guilty."

"Sure, Auntie Lizzie..." *I can't believe my paternal genes are even more screwed up than my maternal's.* "If I'm to take your secret to my grave, would you at least tell me why my mother was blackmailing your brother?" In this day and age, fathering a child out of wedlock wasn't a crime. "The existence of an illegitimate daughter might stain his personal life, but surely it wouldn't threaten his nomination."

Stopped in her tracks, Elisabeth gaped at Willow for what felt like an eternity. "You really don't know the circumstances surrounding your birth, do you?"

Bewildered by her aunt's reaction, Willow almost dreaded hearing the truth. "Neither my mother nor my father ever wanted me, did they?"

"On the contrary, my dear niece, you were very much wanted—until the day you were born."

* * *

In Exam Room One, Zachary adjusted the oxygen mask over the mouth and nose of Willow's grandmother.

"Rose inhaled too much smoke and hit her head, but I'm concerned she also suffered a concussion and other fractures." Angela cleaned the deep cut on the elderly lady's forehead. "She regained consciousness shortly after she was brought in with Nurse Darius. He's in Exam Room Two waiting for you to see him."

Heartened to learn the impostor didn't pose an immediate threat to Willow, Zachary leaned closer to his patient. "Rose? It's Doctor Zachary. Are you hurting anywhere?" Rose gazed at him with glassy eyes. "Angela, we'll start with a chest x-ray, a head scan, and a full blood work. I also want to know if there's any drugs in her system. If she complains about any other injuries, we'll—"

Rose gripped his wrist with a bony hand and ripped her mask with the other. "Brigitte..." Her voice was raspy. "The girl with six toes took Brigitte."

"Brigitte is at peace, Rose." Angela spoke softly. "You can let the doctor go. That's it." The nurse tucked Rose's arm under the blanket then replaced the mask over her face. "We'll take good care of you."

The elderly lady closed her eyes and her breathing evened out.

"It's sad when their mind clocks out before their body." His head nurse opened the suture tray. "I'm thinking butterfly bandage?"

He glanced at the wound. "I'll leave it to your discretion, Angela. Let me know when you have the tests results. I'll be in Exam Room Two."

Before grilling his next patient about Willow's whereabouts, Zachary made a detour by the lobby where he flagged the security guard on duty. "Cain? A word, please?"

"Yes, Dr. Boss?" The new uncle almost saluted him.

Zachary extended a hand. "If you carry handcuffs, I need them."

"Sure." The guard handed them along with a key. "Should I ask what you intend to do with them?"

"I'm about to make a citizen's arrest. I suspect the man pretending to be Nurse Darius Wiedrich blew up my trailer in an attempt to kill me." Zachary hadn't appraised Constable Laforge of the latest developments yet, but he doubted she would bark at his initiative. "I don't want him to flee before the Mounties arrive. You can keep the key."

Cain nodded pocketing the key. "If you don't mind, Doc, I'll stand guard by his door.

You can't be too cautious with guys like him."

Grateful for the additional protection, Zachary entered the second examination room. The man masquerading as a nurse lay unconscious on the bed.

Zachary's first intervention was to cuff his patient's right wrist to the rail. "Now we can proceed."

A quizzical frown scrunched up Nurse Heather's face. "Nurse Darius is strongly sedated, Doc. He isn't going anywhere."

"The real nurse Darius Wiedrich is dead. This man is a dangerous impostor under arrest." Frustrated to be unable to interrogate the impostor right away, Zachary read the firefighters' report. "A medic gave him oxygen at the scene, but he's now breathing on his own and doesn't appear to have suffered any burns. Why is he still sedated?"

"Pain. He screamed in agony when the firefighters moved him." Nurse Heather cut his clothes, exposing a large area of blood engorged tissue beneath the skin on his left side. "That looks bad. No wonder it hurts. A firefighter noticed a lead pipe lying on the floor between the patient and Rose. Could she have taken a swing at him?"

"I doubt she's strong enough to cause that much damage." Zachary palpated the purplish area. Without sedation, his patient wouldn't have withstood the slightest touch, let alone this kind of examination. "I'll need an x-ray to confirm, but it feels like his hip is shattered. Whoever hit him with that pipe meant business... or felt threatened..." A pipe wasn't only a weapon of opportunity, it was also a familiar object to a plumber. The kind of makeshift weapon that Zachary might opt for if he were Willow. "Run a full blood screen and do a hip x-ray but keep him cuffed and sedated. The Mounties will take him into custody when they get here. Do you know if Willow was seen at the nursing home?"

"The fire is still raging but no casualties have been reported so far. All the residents and staff members were evacuated and brought here for a checkup. I have the list of everyone who..." Nurse Heather checked her electronic tablet. "Willow's name is not on the list. If she was at the nursing home, she wasn't brought here."

The words that Rose had muttered gripping his arm resurfaced in Zachary's mind. *The girl with six toes took Brigitte.* In her delusion, Rose often mistook Willow for Brigitte. "Is Elisabeth's name on the list?"

Heather scrolled up and down again. "No. I guess she wasn't there either."

Or she was and she forced Willow to go with her. "Willow wouldn't have abandoned her grandmother on the floor." That much Zachary was certain. "Does Elisabeth still live on Beaver Trail? Or did she move since her last medical visit?"

"Still on Beaver Trail, but you'll rarely find her home. When she isn't at the nursing home, she's at the funeral home."

Zachary extended his hand. "Can I borrow your car, please? It's a matter of life or death."

Chapter 14

Stunned to hear that someone had wanted her, Willow stared in confusion at her aunt. "What changed at my birth that—" The answer took the shape of a finger. An extra finger. "I was rejected because I was born with a lousy sixth finger?"

Elisabeth pushed out a long, noisy breath. "Not exactly."

Frustration built inside Willow. Now that the truth floated within reach, she wanted to grab it and squash it. "Stop beating around the bush, Elisabeth, and have the decency to tell me the truth before you kill me."

"You remind me of me at your age. Spirited and full of life. You're very much a Drewer." Another sly smile flitted across Elisabeth's face. "My parents moved to Ojibson when Doug and I were very young. Dad had an artificial leg. He'd lost the real one in a tractor accident when he was a child, or so he told everyone. The truth is, he was born with six toes, but he'd developed such a bad infection after his father chopped it off that his entire foot had to be amputated. Imagine my mother's shock when I was born with an extra toe. My father was ashamed he'd passed the deformity to me. He didn't want me to be ridiculed like he'd been as a child, but the midwife advised against surgery. All my toes were fully formed, and my foot looked normal. Cutting any toe off would have deformed my foot and affected how I walk. My father eventually yielded to reason..." She rolled her eyes. "After what happened to him, you think he would have been reluctant to put his newborn daughter on the chopping block. Anyway, he was adamant no one should know about it, so I never went barefoot, not even to swim."

It pained Willow that she could relate. "What about your brother?" Zachary had told her that her biological father would have been born with a similar deformity. "Is he hiding a toe or a finger?"

"Finger, but Doug was lucky. The extra digit was just a fleshy lump. No bones. A doctor removed it when he was a baby. You can't see his scar, even if you're looking for it. I see him in you, you know..." Elisabeth scrutinized Willow from head to toes. "Doug's wife Gisele came from money. She could afford anything in life, except the one thing she desired the most. A baby. She was desperate to become a mother, but no procedure in the world could ever allow her to carry a child, so other options were discussed, including surrogacy, which wasn't

253

regulated at the time. I'd noticed Brigitte's uncanny resemblance with Gisele. Your mother was young, barely eighteen, but she already had a reputation of enjoying men's attention and money."

A sordid picture emerged in Willow's mind. "My mother agreed to carry your brother's child, but instead of handing me over, she blackmailed him, didn't she?"

"Not exactly..." Elisabeth's ambiguous responses grated on Willow's nerves. "Doug and Gisele promised to give your mother thirty thousand dollars upon your delivery, and I took care of remunerating Dr. Holloway for his services. Doug drove here to make his sperm donation, but the timing was off. Since Doug couldn't stay and Dr. Holloway didn't have the equipment to freeze his donation, an arrangement was made with a private lab in Ottawa. Doug was to go to that lab where his sperm would be frozen and sent back in a temperature-controlled container, ready to be used at the appropriate moment. Everything was set, but before driving back to Ottawa, Doug insisted on meeting your mother. He wanted to see how much she resembled his wife. Knowing how Brigitte enjoyed enticing men, and how men couldn't resist her charms, I shouldn't have let Doug meet her alone. He spent less than half an hour with her but he still managed to make a *direct* donation."

A sickening scenario hit Willow in the face. "Your brother had sex with my teenage mother upon meeting her?"

"Yes." The sharp acknowledgment spoke of Elisabeth's repressed anger or resentment. "If her insemination had gone as planned, it wouldn't have mattered when or how you were conceived, but the container was damaged during shipping and Doug's sperm was unviable. On your mother's insistence, Dr. Holloway went through the motion of impregnating her, but he didn't want to build Doug's and Gisele's hopes up, so he told them the truth about the damaged shipment. Imagine how surprised we all were when Brigitte became pregnant. Gisele was devastated to learn Brigitte wasn't fit to serve as a surrogate any time soon, but instead of giving up, she became more desperate than ever. Gisele wanted a baby, any baby, at any cost. Boy, girl, white, brown, blue, purple... It no longer mattered if the baby wasn't related to her husband. Set on becoming a mother, Gisele offered to pay Brigitte fifty thousand dollars to give you up for adoption."

"Fifty thousand dollars?" Flabbergasted, Willow ran and reran the number in her head. "My mother turned down *fifty thousand dollars*? No... You're lying. Brigitte would have thrown me off a bridge for half that amount."

"Your mother did agree to sell you, Mitch. She didn't hesitate a second, but when she pushed out a baby with an extra finger, everything went south for everyone involved. If only Dr. Holloway had kept his mouth shut about the unviable sperm shipment, Gisele would have seen the extra finger as a family trait you inherited from the Drewers and taken you home as her daughter. And if you'd been born with normal fingers and toes...." Elisabeth sighed. "Well, your life would have been different. Gisele would have adopted you and the identity of your birth father would have become inconsequential."

The ugly truth dawned on Willow. "Gisele figured out her husband cheated on her with my mother, didn't she? That's why she didn't adopt me." Even in the absence of DNA testing, Willow's extra finger was an undeniable proof of her parentage. "You're blaming my mother for my extra finger, but if your *dear* brother had boosted some willpower and kept his pants on when he met her, we wouldn't be here, would we?"

"Your mother almost ruined his life when she seduced him." Elisabeth's eyes darkened as she raised her voice. "Gisele had forced him to sign a prenup before they married. She was the one with money and influence. Doug knew his wife would never forgive him for fathering a child with another woman. If Gisele had asked for a divorce, he would have lost everything, so he lied. He told her that you were stillborn. Grief-stricken, Gisele never asked for another child, but Doug had to make sure she would never learn the truth. He paid Brigitte to keep his secret, but your mother was greedy. She kept blackmailing him, sending him pictures of your hand. It went on for fifteen years, until the day Gisele died in a boating accident. Doug loved her... he truly loved her, and he was devastated. Banking on his grief and guilty conscience, Brigitte doubled her demands, but that time, she pushed too far. Doug swore to seek sole custody of you if he ever heard of your mother again. He was serious, Mitch, and he was almost disappointed when she backed down. Almost..."

The story shed a different light on the conversation that Willow had overheard almost a decade ago. She *almost* had a better life, except *almost* didn't count. "I'm guessing his recent nomination relit the dollar signs in my mother's eyes and she blackmailed him again?"

"She threatened to expose how he enslaved her into a surrogacy contract, coerced her to have sex with him, and rejected the deformed child that he forced her to carry when she was just a teenager. These were lies, but they still would have destroyed his reputation. He called me... I'm his big sister. I'm supposed to protect him, so I went to see Brigitte. She'd kept her medical record. All the procedures were listed... I begged her not to ruin his career, but she refused to listen. We struggled... After she got stabbed, I trashed her apartment looking for her medical files.

They were in her closet. Now they're ashes."

Elisabeth had killed her mother, but Brigitte would still be alive if greed hadn't lent a helping hand. "Does your brother know you're involved in Brigitte's death? Is he involved in—" An alarm rang in Willow's ears, silencing her.

"Not the security system again. It's the fourth time the cold set it off this week. It's too bad you're a plumber and not an electrician." Elisabeth got up, annoyed. "I'll be back shortly. Don't go anywhere."

* * *

Her sights set on the scalpel resting on the shelf underneath the table, Willow wiggled her buttocks and pushed on the floor with the tip of her boots. The chair screeched on the tiles, marking her slow progress toward the table.

Through gritted teeth, she urged the chair to inch closer, and closer. *Come on.*

Sweat dripped between her shoulders. She hopped to rotate the chair until she came within reach of the scalpel.

Careful not to cut any finger, she grabbed the scalpel backhandedly. The cold metal sent delightful shivers up her arm. *Now the tricky part...*

She placed the blade on the strap binding her wrists together and slowly sliced through it at a snail's pace. *Better a sick and dying snail than a chopped finger.*

After hearing what happened to her paternal grandfather, Willow lost any desire for corrective surgery. For better or worse, she was who she was. Dwelling on who she could have been if one of the dices had rolled differently served no purpose.

The revenge seething inside her deadened heart no longer shot vengeful flames. It now basked into the glowing embers of justice. Brigitte and Nana wouldn't understand, but Zachary would. Unlike them, he valued life above anything, including money. Willow owed it to him, to his memory, not to intentionally take someone's life. *You were the best thing that ever happened to me, Zachary Auckerman.*

The strap snapped, and she lost her grip on the scalpel.

She hurried to untie the bindings from her ankles, then bolted to her feet. The scalpel had tumbled near the leg of the chair. It would make a deadly weapon at close range, but determined to avoid a physical confrontation, Willow scanned the room for a longer weapon, something like a lead pipe, a tire iron, a baseball bat, a—

A fire extinguisher rested on the floor near an open and empty wooden coffin.

That would make a good weapon. The arrow on the gauge of the fire extinguisher was in the green octant. She picked it up and pulled off the safety pin. *You better be working. My life literally depends on you.*

Silence filled the air.

The security system had been deactivated. It was only a matter of minutes before Elisabeth returned. Her aunt hadn't carried any weapon that Willow could see, but still reeling from the last jab that had incapacitated her, she intended to strike first.

With no place to hide in the chamber, Willow tiptoed up the staircase. A loud thud resonated in her ears, jolting her senses on high alert. She stopped at the top of the stairs and peeked around the door that had been left ajar.

Two legs lay on the floor and they both ended with brown loafers.

Someone incapacitated Elisabeth? Willow's first thought was for Cedric Lynch. *If you're seeking revenge on Elisabeth, I won't stop you, but you better let me go.*

Ready to blast her way to freedom, Willow placed a finger on the trigger of the fire extinguisher, and aiming ahead, she elbowed the door wide open.

At the sight of Zachary hunched over Elisabeth, Willow gasped in shock. The fire extinguisher slipped from her hand.

"Careful!" Zachary lunged toward her, grabbed her by the shoulders, and pulled her against his chest.

The fire extinguisher grazed her boot hitting the floor.

"Zachary?" His trailer was blown to

smithereens seconds after he'd returned home. He couldn't have escaped such a deadly explosion. Nobody could. "You're... you're dead. I saw the explosion..."

"The mice saved me." He stroked her back holding her close. "Are you injured? Did she hurt you?"

"No... I don't think so..." The strong heartbeat against her ear grounded her to reality. "Nana? Lynch set a fire. We have—"

The tender kiss he bestowed on her forehead tied her tongue. "Your grandmother is safe, Willow. I promise to recount everything, but first I need your help restraining Elisabeth. I think I sprained my hand punching her."

* * *

Spinning from the events that turned her life upside down, Willow slumped on the armchair by her grandmother's hospital bed.

Recounting all the incriminating statements that Elisabeth Brown and Cedric Lynch made in her presence had drained Willow. Her verbal account was corroborated by the documents found in the archive of the hospital and Zachary's interactions with both culprits. The doctor had figured out the circumstances surrounding her birth, but not the correct identity of the couple who wanted her but couldn't have her because of her extra finger.

Whoever said *money talks* was wrong. Money didn't talk, it lied.

After recording her deposition, Constable Laforge had assured Willow that she wouldn't face any consequences for hitting Cedric Lynch with a pipe in self-defense.

Unlike Elisabeth, Lynch would need more than a good lawyer, he would also need a terrific orthopedic surgeon.

They reaped what they sowed. For as long as Willow lived, she never wanted to see either one of them again.

Her grandmother shared her hospital room with Agnes, the resident who unwittingly kept the drug paraphernalia in her bathroom. The fire had caused damage to the nursing room but no casualties. The elderly ladies snored in tandem, their loud performance attesting to their recovery.

Rocked by the comforting noise, Willow drifted back and forth between dreams, nightmares, and reality.

"Willow?"

Caresses on her forearm drew a gentle but clear path toward reality. She opened her eyes and smiled. "Is it broken?"

After giving his deposition to Laforge, Zachary had left to get an x-ray. His right hand didn't sport a cast, but it was wrapped in a bandage.

"Sprained." His five o'clock shadow accentuated his weary expression.

"Punching someone isn't as easy, or painless, as they make it appear in the movies."

"Nothing is as easy as it is in the movies." However, owing one's life to the mice infesting a trailer and the traps kept in a shed by an unscrupulous landlord was an incredible and fortunate twist. "On the other hand, the explosion of your trailer broke your lease."

"Yeah, except I'm homeless. Again." Zachary leaned his hip against the ledge of the window. "We need to talk about the incident that created a rift between us. It wasn't what you think it was."

"I know..." Willow briefly closed her eyes to revisit the only event to which he could refer. "The hood of her car was still warm despite the frigid temperature. She couldn't have been in your trailer more than ten minutes, but when I saw her wrapped in a towel I... I was shocked and I came to the wrong conclusion, not that it should have mattered. You were allowed to date or have dinner with whoever you wished. The two weren't mutually exclusive."

"As a man and a doctor, I disagree." A smile crinkled the corners of his eyes and chased away his fatigue. "There's barely enough hours in my day to date one woman, let alone two at the same time. Besides, why would I risk losing the most amazing woman I've ever met?"

Thunderstruck by his last few words, Willow stared at him searching for a different meaning than the one her heart conjured up.

The door swung open, and the nurse who'd wreaked havoc with Willow's heart entered.

"Angela said you wanted to see me, Doc?" Camille's sweet and innocent demeanor vanished the moment she laid eyes on Willow. "Mitch? I wasn't aware you were visiting your grandmother. I can come back later."

"No, your timing is perfect." Zachary gestured for the nurse to approach. "I was about to tell Willow how you offered to hang my coat but managed to lose my keys for a few hours. Interestingly enough, Chester sent me a picture of you and Willow standing on the porch of my trailer during that timeframe." Zachary's gaze, directed solely at the nurse, had lost its warmth. "I thought I made it clear when you asked me out that I didn't fraternize with my nurses."

The pretty nurse rolled on her heels, her expression inscrutable. "I didn't have any hot water at home, and you weren't home, so I didn't think you'd mind if I took a shower."

Willow choked on the lame excuse but managed to hide her disbelief behind the timely clearing of her throat. "When you texted me for a service call saying you ran out of hot water, you meant at your house, not at the doctor's?"

"Of course." Camille shot invisible daggers out of her eyes, all of them aiming straight at Willow's chest. "It's not my fault you misread my text."

"Listen very attentively, *Nurse* Camille." Zachary straightened his back. "My private life is out of bound. If anyone attempts to sabotage my personal relationship with Willow, he—or she—will regret their actions. Are we crystal clear this time?"

Camille pursed her lips together. "Like I said, *Doctor,* it was an unfortunate misunderstanding, but from now on, I suggest you hang your coat yourself. I'm a nurse, not a valet." On these last words, Camille turned on her heels and walked out.

Stunned by her brisk departure, Willow glanced back and forth between Zachary and the slowly closing door. "She lied, ambushed me, and blamed *you*? What reality does she live in?"

"I was once warned that she lived in a reality where she gets everything she wants, but that was an understatement." He rubbed his face with both hands. "I know that discussion might have been better served in private, but since you both appeared in the photo that Chester tried to blackmail me with, it concerned you both. Besides, I doubted these two elderly ladies would mind." Their snoring cut through the air he'd cleared with a chainsaw. "I remember how I felt when I learned my ex-girlfriend cheated on me. It's not something I wish on anyone. I'm sorry for the embarrassment and pain that Nurse Camille put you through, Willow.

I'm guessing she gave you quite a performance?"

"An award-winning performance." The shock of seeing the nurse half-naked had blurred the inconsistencies, like the warm hood and Camille's dry hair, and cast a shadow on Zachary's character. "She should have been an actress instead of a nurse, but I should have remembered you're not like my late husband, or the men in my mother's life."

"No offense, but your mother set a low bar." He took her hand, the one that sealed her fate, and gently caressed it with his thumb. "You deserve a good and decent man in your life, Willow. I'm not perfect, far from it, but I try to be the kind of man I would wish for my daughter one day. If there's a chance you could live with a man who loves you very much and thinks of you all the time despite spending lots of evenings and weekends in his second home, and by second home I mean the hospital not a cozy cottage by a lake, then that man would very much like to have dinner with you."

Tears pooled in her eyes. Zachary might not be perfect, but he embodied everything Willow valued, everything she ever wanted in a man but never thought she would find—or deserved to find.

"I heard there was a guy in town whose trailer blew up. I could let him stay in my spare room until he finds a new place, but he would need to help me declutter it. On the bright side, it's mouse-free and I could even feed him from time to time," she teased, emboldened by the glow in his eyes. "If he were to live under my roof, I might be able to see him an extra ten minutes every day... it's almost long enough to be called daily dating."

His laughter filled the room. "You hooked that lucky guy with *mouse-free* and—"

The door swung open, and Angela peeked inside the room. "Chainsaw accident."

Willow reluctantly nudged him away. "Someone needs you, Doc." His heart might belong to her, but she had to accept she would always share him with his patients. "Go do your job."

Zachary kissed her then left the room.

Chapter 15

Five months later

After a satisfying day installing plumbing in a new house, Willow returned home in time for supper.

In the living room, her grandmother rocked in her glider chair by the fireplace.

"That's the end of the chapter, Rose. We'll continue reading Seasoned Hearts tomorrow." Mrs. Diamond, one of the three attendants providing round-the-clock care for Nana, set her latest mystery novel on the coffee table. "Now that your granddaughter is back, I'll give you a nice warm scented bath. You haven't had one in two days. You'll feel so good slipping in a clean nightgown."

Her grandmother pouted. "I don't like the bath."

"I know you don't like the bath, Nana, but you love smelling like lavender, don't you?" Willow positioned herself on one side of the glider chair while Mrs. Diamond took the other side. "It's bubble time."

Together they lifted Nana and carried her up the stairs into the second-floor bathroom, the only bathroom in the house with a bathtub.

"Thank you, Mitch." Once they settled Nana on the seat of her upstairs walker, Mrs. Diamond took over. "I'll shout when we're ready to come down, but it won't be for at least half an hour. Rose has a rash on her buttocks and it'll do her good to spend some time soaking in Epson Salt."

"You're a gem, Mrs. Diamond. Take as long as you need. I'll be in the kitchen making supper." Willow couldn't have hoped for better attendants, but unfortunately none of them was strong enough to carry Nana up the stairs on their own. Her grandmother only got a full bath when Willow or Zachary were available to help.

After being forced to bring Nana home, Willow had transformed her grandmother's sewing room on the main floor into a large bedroom and furnished it with a hospital bed and a cot in case the attendant felt like lying down. A bathroom equipped with a sink and a toilet was already located on the main floor, but it was too small to add a tub or a shower stall. *It's too bad that Nana didn't have the foresight to buy a bungalow instead of a two-story house.*

Upon entering the kitchen, Willow turned on the radio then took a bag of ready-to-eat lettuce, some carrots, a green pepper, and a roasted chicken out of the fridge.

—is Artie Denzel with your six o'clock news. Amanda is sick, so I'll be your host for the evening.

More than five months after a fire forced the evacuation of the nursing home and the relocation of its twenty-four residents, the final report of the lengthy inspection of the building dashed their hopes of ever returning.

"None of the residents were eager to return, Artie." Willow's feelings toward the nursing home resonated louder than the chopping sound her knife made on the cutting board.

The sprinkler system had failed. If not for the timely arrival of the firefighters, the fire would have completely destroyed the kitchen wing. Willow was still amazed they were able to extract her grandmother and Lynch before they died. The inspection had also uncovered an outdated electrical system, serious structural damages, and many other issues mostly related to the age and the lack of maintenance of the building.

The building will have to be demolished before anything else is built in its site, but there's hope on the horizon

for the families struggling to
care for their elderly relatives.

After the fire, the residents requiring the most urgent care were moved to facilities hours away from Ojibson. Still, more than two-thirds of them ended up back home.

If not for the wonderful attendants that Willow could afford to hire, she had no idea how she would cope. Unlike many others suddenly forced to care for elderly relatives, Willow was lucky, but the irony that she owed her peace of mind to Brigitte wasn't lost on her.

The Health Department announced the creation of a temporary long-term care wing in the basement of the hospital. The wing will consist of ten double occupancy rooms able to accommodate up to twenty patients. Priority will be given to the former residents of the nursing home.

I heard from good authority that the wing could open as early as the end of the week.

"No, Artie, it won't open by Friday. The new beds won't arrive until next week and they haven't finished hiring additional staff to take care of these elderly patients yet." A slice of carrot flew into the air and landed on her sock. Willow tossed it in the garbage.

> *On a legal front, the saga of Elisabeth Brown, owner and former director of the nursing home, continues. More charges were added against her. It is alleged she hired a felon to murder her husband, John Brown. For the listeners who are too young to remember, John died in the fire that consumed the Moose Pub, the Antlers Pub predecessor, almost twenty years ago.*

"Who would have thought that trying to murder the only son of your hitman would untie his tongue?" That irony made Willow's smile.

Zachary and Constable Laforge were in Cedric Lynch's hospital room when he called his father to tell him that Elisabeth had left him to die in the fire. Fergus Lynch wasn't just livid, he was also on speaker. He spilled the beans on his contract killing, not in exchange for a better prison term, but to make certain Elisabeth would rot in jail for the rest of her life.

According to Fergus Lynch's statement, John Brown was a rich and taciturn man that Elisabeth charmed into marrying her, but he wasn't stupid. He'd tied all his financial wealth to his funeral home and made sure his wife wouldn't be entitled to any money if she divorced him before their twenty-fifth wedding anniversary. Quickly bored by a middled-aged husband who showed more interest in cold bodies than warm ones, Elisabeth began having affairs during her trips to see her brother Doug. She met Fergus Lynch in a bar in Ottawa, they hit it off, and when she shared her desire to get rid of her husband, he agreed to take care of her problem in exchange of a lump sum payment. Fergus instigated the brawl, beat John unconscious then set the pub on fire to finish him off and burn any evidence of his murder. Elisabeth inherited John's funeral home and money, Fergus got paid, and they went their separate ways.

Learning her paternal aunt had only married John Brown for his money hadn't come as a shock to Willow. Both sides of her family were equally greedy. "I bet you were anything but pleasantly surprised when Fergus contacted you last summer and brought up the past, were you, Elisabeth?"

Cedric, Fergus's secret son, was a paramedic who'd double-crossed a drug dealer. After his shady deal backfired, Cedric was forced to go into hiding. Fast. His father arranged for him to borrow the identity of a recently deceased nurse that Fergus had befriended during his many visits to the prison infirmary. Darius Wiedrich. Then

Fergus contacted his former lover Elisabeth and threatened to reveal the details of her husband's death if she didn't help his son. Elisabeth reluctantly harbored the new Darius and gave him a legitimate job, except he was supposed to keep a low profile—not build a drug lab or start eliminating residents. "If you'd stayed out of trouble, Cedric, the subsequent events probably wouldn't have occurred, and everyone's secrets might have remained safe."

Elisabeth Brown has been released on bail and will be trialed later this year. However, the unnamed nurse who participated in Brown's alleged other crimes at the nursing home, has reached a plea deal. The details were not made public, but it will undoubtedly shave years off his sentence and cause major headaches for Brown's defense lawyer.

Her legal issues prompted her brother, Judge Douglass Drewer, to issue a statement in which he condemned violence and deplored her aberrant behavior. He also announced his early retirement. Drewer could have served many more years

at the Court of Appeal, but
some of his critics argued that
his sister's conviction, or
acquittal, would have cast a
shadow on his tenure.

"Elisabeth doesn't have a defense, but that's not his sister's conviction that the judge dreads. He's afraid of what may be revealed in court concerning *my* birth."

A month ago, Willow had received an unexpected phone call from Douglass Drewer. At first, he'd showed guarded interest in her, but his concerns quickly shifted to any contentious allegations that Brigitte might have made against him over the years, and to any existing documents that could lend credibility to such allegations. After Willow admitted knowing about the surrogacy arrangement, he attempted to buy her silence. Hurt and offended by the presumption she would play her mother's game, Willow had hung up, severing all ties with her paternal side.

In other news, folks, we
have an old mystery to solve.
I'm sure you've all seen the
bright yellow flyers that have
popped up at the hospital, the
post office, and almost on
every lamppost around town
in the last few days. If the
voracious mosquitoes have

stopped you from venturing outside, or if you just haven't paid attention, please go to our website. The flyer is on our main page. It's important that anyone fifty and older takes a good look at the young man pictured on the flyer.

The RCMP believe this young man visited Ojibson in the months prior to his death forty-five years ago. Yes, folks, forty-five years ago. That's a very cold case, so let's warm it up. There's no rewards if you recognize him. That young man didn't commit any crimes, but because he didn't carry any I.D. when he died in a car accident, he was buried without a name, and his poor family was never notified. That, folks, is sad. Very sad.

So, if you think you recognize that young man from long ago, call the radio station or Constable Laforge at the RCMP detachment.

"Thanks for your help, Artie." DNA testing had confirmed the unknown young man was indeed her maternal grandfather, but after months of showing his picture to anyone in town, Willow still hadn't uncovered his identity.

It appeared more and more likely that her grandmother had met her young lover anywhere but in Ojibson. Still, before giving up, Willow had asked Constable Laforge's permission to plaster the town with flyers in a last-ditch effort to identify him.

The back door opened.

Zachary stepped in wearing a lab coat over his pale blue scrubs. "Hello, luv."

His greeting awoke the butterflies in her stomach. "I wasn't expecting you until seven." She lowered the knife on the cutting board, and after meeting him halfway, she laced her fingers behind his neck. "Didn't you have Zoom interviews to conduct tonight?"

"I still do, but they are delayed. There was a time zone mix-up in the scheduling." Zach wrapped her in his arms and peppered light kisses on her lips, cooking up delicious sensations all over her body. "I thought I'd take advantage of my break to come home and enjoy a quick supper with you. How was your day?"

"Smooth and problem-free." Installing new plumbing was a breeze compared with replacing old ones. "The bathrooms in that new house I'm working on will be gorgeous." She basked in his warm embrace, wishing for time to slow down. "I'm making a chicken salad, but there's a shepherd's pie leftover in the fridge. I can reheat it if you're in a rush and make something else for Nana." Her grandmother ate like a bird despite clamoring to be starving and complained about the food regardless of what Willow served her. Trying to satisfy Nana's tastebuds was a losing battle. "She's taking a long bath right now."

"The shepherd's pie will be easier for Rose to eat. I can wait for the salad." He released her and removed his lab coat. "Guess who decided to quit today?"

Please, not Angela. "Who?"

"Camille." A smirk tugged at his lips. "Remember me telling you about the doctor at Kingston General? The one who gave me misleading information about the real nurse Darius?"

"Yes..." Confused about where or how Camille fit in that story, Willow resumed chopping vegetables. "Didn't you hire one of his nurses a few weeks back? The one that set the record straight about the real Darius?"

"Yes, Nurse Martha Beckett. After she resigned, Camille applied for Martha's old position in the geriatric department." The amusement in his voice was unmistakable. "Camille starts next week. Apparently Dr. Crocker is delighted to have her on board."

"I bet he is." *Talk about Karma with a capital K.* "I wonder how long Camille will appreciate his attention." More or less indifferent to Camille's fate, Willow dumped the chopped vegetables into a bowl, added the lettuce, then proceeded to cut a chicken breast into cubes. "Should I be jealous of Nurse Martha? Should I wonder if you sneaked your way onto the hiring committee just to hire her?"

His laughter resonated in the kitchen. "I wasn't supposed to be on any hiring committee, luv, but I'll admit it's nice to have a say on who will come to work at the hospital. Nurse Martha will be a great addition to the staff, and her wife is a nutritionist, so we're negotiating with her as well. They have two young kids. I'm looking forward to introducing them to you. We have two more positions to fill before we can open the geriatric wing... I can't say I'm overly impressed by the resumés left on my desk, but maybe one of them will stand out during the interviews this evening."

* * *

The heavy rain forecast for the next few days prompted Willow to remove what was left of the flyers posted outdoor before they become a soggy mush of pulp and littered the sidewalks.

She tossed them in her recycling bin, disappointed that the many new leads forwarded to Constable Laforge in the last two weeks failed to identify the clean-shaven young man who'd fathered Brigitte.

279

In the last six months, Willow had added many names to the branches of her pathetic family tree. She accepted that the branch belonging to her maternal grandfather might forever remain nameless. Still, like Artie had said on the radio, it was sad that his family was never notified of his death. Everyone deserved closure.

She entered the kitchen where a plate of homemade cookies on the middle of the table caught her attention. Double chocolate chip cookies were her favorite. Willow selected the biggest of all and took a huge bite. Slowly chewing, she fully enjoyed the flavor caressing her tastebuds.

"I see you found my mother's cookies." Mrs. Diamond chuckled joining Willow in the kitchen. "She baked them for your grandmother after she talked to the RCMP constable this morning, but I'm afraid Rose ate one too many before lunch. She hardly touched her oatmeal before taking her nap. She's soundly asleep right now."

"Your mother's cookies are delicious. Besides, any food that makes it in Nana's stomach is better than no food at all." At her age, her grandmother might as well enjoy eating what she liked best. *It's not like Nana has that many years left.* "May I ask if your mother is okay? She wasn't victim of a crime, was she?"

"Oh no, nothing like that. It's the guy on the yellow flyers. She thought he looked familiar, but she just couldn't place him, then at three in the morning, *his eyes* woke her up." Mrs. Diamond rolled her eyes. "As you know, my mother lives with us, but why she felt the need to also wake me up instead of waiting at a reasonable time to tell me, I'll never know. Anyway, talking to the constable had reminded her of your grandmother, so she decided to bake a batch of cookies while I was trying to get my kids ready for school. It was a chaotic morning to say the least."

"Your mother recognized him?" Heartened by this new lead, Willow grabbed a second cookie. "What did she say about him?"

"Apparently he had a beard back then, that's why she said she didn't recognize him right away, but there was something about his eyes that suddenly triggered her memory." Mrs. Diamond shrugged filling up the kettle. "I never knew your grandmother was my mother's teacher in high school. Not until this morning that is. Anyway, if my mother is correct, the man on the flyers was the student-teacher who taught English in your grandmother's class for a few weeks." A chuckle escaped her lips. "Mom loved his Irish accent when he read poetry. I got the feeling she might have had a teenage crush on him."

Brigitte was the product of Nana's liaison with a student-teacher under her tutelage? Appalled, Willow shoved the entire cookie in her mouth. Didn't any of her relatives know how to behave accordingly? Apparently not. "Does your mother remember his name?"

"She'd given him the nickname Elliot Ness, but she couldn't recall his exact name. The constable said she would look into it." Mrs. Diamond proceeded to place two mugs on the table. "Would you like a cup of tea?"

"A chamomile tea would be nice. Thank you." *If the student-teacher only stayed in Ojibson a few weeks, Nana may not have known she was pregnant by the time he left, but she may have wondered why he never came back.*

In an ironic twist of fate, Rose and Brigitte might have been denied the same thing they'd denied Willow all these years. Truth and closure.

* * *

Unable to sleep, Willow stared at the shadows dancing in the window. She never lowered the blinds, not because she feared darkness, but because they would unravel, and she would need to replace them. That way she could ignore the looming expense.

Tonight, a full moon played hide-and-seek among the clouds. The branches of the evergreen growing in her yard danced in the wind. The sight soothed her mind.

A door opened and closed.

He climbed upstairs. The fourth step creaked under his weight, but the rest of his steps were muffled by the worn-out carpet.

Willow had briefly seen him at suppertime but she missed his good night kiss. "I'm awake. How was your evening?"

"Busy." Zachary quietly entered the bedroom. "We admitted Agnes Goose tonight. Her daughter-in-law did an incredible job taking care of her, but she brought in Agnes in the nick of time. We only had one bed left. Now our temporary long-term care wing is officially at full capacity."

"I know it was a team effort, but you deserve an accolade for coming up with the idea of a geriatric wing and turning it into reality." Without Zachary's relentless effort and determination, the former residents would still be waiting to receive the kind and compassionate care they all deserved. "I got a call from Constable Laforge while I was taking a bath. Brigitte's father was Elliot McGuiness, a twenty-one-year-old student-teacher who did a short practicum in Nana's classroom. He grew up in a farming community in southern Saskatchewan, but his family didn't report him missing until a few years later. Now that my family tree is complete, I'm thinking of chopping it down, selling the house, and leaving all the bad memories behind."

"Easy with the axe, luv." In the moonlight, Zachary's fatigue faded, replaced by soft contentment. "There's a special branch that I love with all my heart, but I'll admit I've been toying with the idea of buying a new house."

"You want to move out?" In the last few months, he'd spent more nights in her bedroom than in the guestroom, and Willow could have sworn he enjoyed the arrangement.

"Not just me, luv. All of us." He sat at the edge of the bed. "You deserve to live in a house that don't require fixing every week. Rose needs a bedroom on the main level with a full bathroom suite. And I wouldn't mind an office den, bigger closets, a double attached garage... and a few children's bedrooms." He took her hand into his. "I love you, Willow. I want to make a life with you in Ojibson and I want our children to grow up here. I know your first marriage didn't end well, but it would mean a lot to me if you were willing to give marriage one last chance."

Tears pooled in her eyes. "I love the blueprint of that wonderful life you're promising me, Zachary Auckerman." This was her secret dream, the dream she kept hidden deep in her heart. "House, marriage, and children. I love it all, and I love you."

"You're making me a very happy man, Willow Mitchell." He lay next to her and wrapped her in his arms. "If we were to act soon, our wedding could be a fall affair and our dream home could become reality by next summer." He teased her lips with light kisses. "I will however leave the selection of your ring and the timing of our children to you since you're the one who will wear it and carry them."

The man who taught her and showed her the real meaning of love was her future. At peace with her past, she grabbed that amazing future with both hands and fingers. All eleven of them.

The End

J. S. Marlo grew up in Shawinigan, a small French-Canadian town in Quebec. She attended military college for a year, then married a young officer and raised three spirited children. Over the years, she enjoyed many wonderful postings in many different parts of Canada.

She isn't sure where time flew, but decades later, she ended up under the Northern Lights where she and her hubby are spoiling four wonderful grandchildren.

J. S. Marlo's books also published by BWL Publishing

Wounded Hearts
Seasoned Hearts
The Red Quilt
Mishandled Conviction
Misguided Honor
Voted Out